groucho Marx and
the Broadway Murders

Also by **Ron Goulart**

Elementary, My Dear Groucho
Groucho Marx, Private Eye
Groucho Marx, Master Detective

groucho Marx and the Broadway Murders

Ron Goulart

Thomas Dunne Books
St. Martin's Minotaur ✹ New York

THOMAS DUNNE BOOKS.
An imprint of St. Martin's Press.

GROUCHO MARX AND THE BROADWAY MURDERS. Copyright © 2001 by
Groucho Marx Productions Inc. and Ron Goulart. All rights reserved.
Printed in the United States of America. No part of this book may be
used or reproduced in any manner whatsoever without written permission except in the case of brief quotations embodied in critical arti-
cles or reviews. For information, address St. Martin's Press, 175 Fifth
Avenue, New York, N.Y. 10010.

www.minotaurbooks.com

Library of Congress Cataloging-in-Publication Data

Goulart, Ron.
        Groucho Marx and the Broadway Murders / Ron Goulart.—
1st ed.
            p. cm.
        ISBN 0-312-26598-0
        1. Marx, Groucho, 1891–1977—Fiction. 2. Broadway
(New York, N.Y.)—Fiction. 3. Comedians—Fiction.
4. Theater—Fiction. I Title

PS3557.O85 G75 2001
813'.54—dc21

                                                    2001019157

First Edition: July 2001

10   9   8   7   6   5   4   3   2   1

To Fran, Sean, and Steffan once again

Thanks once more to Robert Finkelstein for his continued cooperation.

groucho Marx and the Broadway Murders

One

Groucho Marx solved his first Manhattan murder case in the summer of 1939.

For good measure, again with me as his Watson, he also managed to solve a killing that had taken place in Hollywood. That we did from a distance of some three thousand miles.

I'm Frank Denby. I used to be a crime reporter with the *Los Angeles Times*. Two years before, while I was scripting Groucho's weekly radio show, he and I became a detective team for the first time and came up with the solution to a murder. Since then we'd worked successfully on several other cases. "We're as good as the Thin Man, Philo Vance, and Charlie Chan rolled into one," Groucho maintained. "Although why anybody would want a five-hundred-pound detective is beyond me."

After our radio show was cancelled, Groucho and I collaborated on a screwball comedy movie script we called *Cinderella on Wheels*. That had been optioned by Mammoth Pictures and was presently languishing on the shelf. But on the strength of that sale, I managed to get myself hired for six months as a staff writer at Mammoth. Working in an impressively small office in the Writers' Building, I initially turned out a revise on the script for *Curse of the Zombies* and then did the second draft of *The Zombies Walk Again*. "That's not a catchy enough title for upper-crust patrons such as myself," Groucho had observed on hearing it. "Nobody *walks* in Beverly Hills. You'd best rechristen it *The Zombies Ride Again, Preferably in a Rolls-Royce.*"

I next wrote the first two drafts on *Stop the Presses,* a B movie that Mammoth was trying to get either Chester Morris or Lee Tracy—whoever'd work more cheaply—to star in. Hollywood being Hollywood, none of these movies was a comedy. My contract hadn't been picked up and by early summer I was once again at liberty. But I was in no danger of starving.

My wife, Jane, is the best-looking cartoonist in America and her comic strip, *Hollywood Molly,* was by then the third most popular in the country. As a result, a large New York advertising agency and the Amalgamated Radio Network wanted to talk to her about turning *Molly* into a weekly radio show. When they suggested that Jane come back to Manhattan to discuss the idea and the possibility of writing the scripts herself, she told them she wouldn't be interested at all unless she could collaborate with her gifted author husband. So we'd both been invited eastward.

Admittedly I was moderately depressed by the fact that I had—temporarily I hoped—ceased to contribute to the family income. And I wasn't any too cheered by the way things in general were going with the world. Franco's gang had won the civil war in Spain, adding another fascist dictator to the list. Hitler was continuing to take over more and more of Europe and both England and France seemed on the brink of declaring war on Germany. President Roosevelt was still talking about keeping America out of World War II, but I figured we were going to get into it fairly soon.

Two days before we were booked to leave on the Super Chief streamliner out of the brand-new Union Station, I decided to stop in at Groucho's Sunset Strip office to tell him that we'd be out of town for a couple of weeks.

It was a clear, blue afternoon and the traffic flashing by on Sunset was the usual mix of foreign sports cars, limousines, and jalopies. As I walked toward the building in which Groucho rented office space, I passed three

2

separate young women who bore an uncanny resemblance to the late Jean Harlow. The building itself resembled a Poverty Row set designer's idea of a Southern mansion.

I was halfway up the wooden stairs that led to the second floor when I heard a loud rattling thump from the vicinity of Groucho's outer office.

Double-timing, I hurried up to the door and yanked it open.

Nan Somerville, his secretary, was sprawled on the floor next to her desk. She was just starting to sit up, muttering. Half of a torn theatrical poster was clutched in her right hand. "Hi, Frank," she said. "Never stand on a swivel chair when you're ripping the poster of a no-good magician off your office wall."

Leaning over, I took hold of her free hand and helped her to rise. "Sound advice," I said. "In fact, wasn't that something Benjamin Franklin included in *Poor Richard's Almanac?*"

"Quite probably, although every time I ran into Ben Franklin all he ever told me was to go fly a kite."

"Sounds like you're coming down with Grouchoitis."

"God, I hope not. Did that really sound like a line he'd say?"

"Or already said."

"Oy."

Nan was a feisty, muscular lady in her late thirties and her earlier career as a circus acrobat and then a stuntwoman at MGM convinced Groucho she would be ideally suited to work as his secretary. She was a crackerjack typist, too.

Glancing up at the portion of the poster that was still on the wall, I inquired, "You and Young Houdini have broken up?"

She crumpled up her portion of the poster and tossed it into the deskside wastebasket. "I should've known any guy of forty-six who calls himself Young anything was going to be untrustworthy."

"So what precipitated the breakup?" I looked at the closed door of Groucho's inner office.

"Groucho wasn't to blame for this one," she said. "Admittedly he scared the Amazing El Carim off by insisting on doing card tricks for him

3

every time he dropped by here to pick me up for lunch. And he alienated Yarko the Great by repeatedly warning him that I was too heavy to be used safely in his Floating Lady illusion. But he didn't screw the Young Houdini romance up."

Nan, a mostly rational person otherwise, had an unfortunate affinity for falling in love only with guys who were professional magicians.

"What exactly happened?"

"Young Houdini vanished."

"Magicians," I pointed out, "have a tendency to do that now and then."

"True, but not with two hundred dollars of my money."

"You didn't loan the guy dough?"

"He borrowed it," Nan corrected. "Although I didn't know that until I consulted the cookie jar in my kitchen two nights ago. The money and Young Houdini haven't been seen since."

After a sympathetic nod, I asked her, "Groucho in?"

Nan pointed a thumb in the direction of the Sunset Strip. "Across the street at Moonbaum's deli," she said. "How's Jane?"

"You may find this hard to believe, but she's doing better than I am."

Nan sat down in the swivel chair and rested her elbows on her desk. "You still don't like the idea that she makes enough money to support you if need be, do you?"

"I can live with it, but—"

"Jane's not the usual wife, so you're really going to have to get used to that fact."

"I suppose so, yeah," I said. "She and I are going to be heading back East in a couple of days and I dropped in to say farewell to Groucho."

"Vacation? Second honeymoon?"

"Nope, mostly business." And I explained about the radio show deal.

"Gee, that's swell," said Nan when I finished. "It'll be, I bet, more fun collaborating with your wife than with Groucho."

"I'm undecided about that," I told her, moving to the door. "I've become used to cigar smoke."

4

"Have a safe trip," said Nan.

"B movies to the contrary," I assured her, "nothing very exciting or dangerous ever happens on a train trip east."

At the time I actually believed that.

There was a chunky forty-year-old newsboy in a Hawaiian shirt hawking papers out in front of the deli. "Extra! Extra!" he was shouting. "Mobster killed in gangland slaying!"

The gangster in question was a local gambler named Nick Sanantonio. I hadn't the faintest suspicion that his violent death had a damn thing to do with me.

I found Groucho in his favorite booth, looking forlornly from his blintzes to a thick manuscript opened beside his plate. "I've been blintzkrieged," he complained as I slid in opposite him. "Mellman the waiter persuaded me to peruse his latest play."

"This isn't still *The Rape of the Lox*, is it?"

"Nay, this is a new effort of his." Groucho gave a negative shake of his head. "I entered these sacred confines simply to indulge in a helping of cheese blintzes and a celery tonic and then Mellman descended on me like a snappy simile I'll think of before we go to press. He pleaded with me to read this new effort, which is entitled something like *Shootout at Kosher Canyon* or *Goodbye, Mr. Knish* or—"

"No, Groucho, it's called *Love Laughs at Lox Myths*," corrected the lean, frail Mellman, who'd been lurking nearby.

"Begone," suggested Groucho, making a shooing motion. "My disciple and I have some parables to whip into shape. Then, if we have time, I want to revise my Sermon on the Mount and put in some more socko one-liners. We're also thinking of picking a new location for that—how's the Sermon at Malibu strike you?"

"I'll bring you some more coffee." The waiter went flat-footing away.

I leaned an elbow on the tabletop and said, "The reason I dropped by, Groucho, was—"

5

"You haven't even asked me, Rollo, why I have such a woebegone expression on my puss."

"I mistook it for your everyday look. Sorry."

"The reason is that I saw the final cut of *At the Circus* yesterday."

"And?"

"Chico, Harpo, and I have pretty much decided to change our name to the Andrews Sisters and try starting all over again."

The Marx Brothers had just recently finished filming a new movie for MGM. It was part of a three-picture deal for which they were being handsomely paid. I mentioned that to Groucho.

"Actually, my lad, the salary goes beyond handsomely and into gorgeously," he corrected. "When you realize that three overgrown street urchins are pulling down such dough, why, it makes you proud to be an American. If only *At the Circus* wasn't so out and out lousy, I'm sure we'd all be as happy as kings. The kings I have in mind are, reading from left to right, King Lear, Wayne King, and King of the Royal Mounted." He paused to fish a cigar out of the pocket of his corn-colored sports coat. "Now, many of our critics think we'll go from bad to worse with these three movies. But we've outwitted them by making the worst one first. So what we'll be doing is going from worse to bad."

"I thought you were pleased to be back at Metro-Goldwyn-Mayer."

"In your vanished youth did you see a film entitled *Frankenstein*?"

"Sure, but—"

"How about a cinematic effort called *The Mummy*?"

"Yeah."

"What do those two movies have in common?"

"Boris Karloff?"

"No, Rollo. The monsters in both were based on Louis B. Mayer," he said, putting the dead cigar between his teeth. "And Mayer is still roaming the grounds at MGM. At night the peasants claim they can hear him howling at the moon, pinching starlets, and dropping options."

"Can I mention now why I—"

"Here's something else to think about on those sleepless nights at the front," he continued. "On its roster of stars MGM has such beauties as Greta Garbo, Hedy Lamarr, Myrna Loy, Jeanette MacDonald, and Eleanor Powell. But who was cast as the young thing I make a pass at?"

"Wasn't Eve Arden in that movie with you?"

"Exactly." He dropped the unlit cigar away in his coat pocket and returned his attention to his blintzes. "But enough evasion, old chap. Tell me why you intruded on my humble repast?"

"Jane and I are leaving for New York this Thursday and—"

"I forgot to mention that there are actually two highly passable moments in *At the Circus*." He ate the final bite. "Modesty prevents me from saying that I'm responsible for both. However, since you're obviously about to plead and cajole, I'll reveal that one occurs when I appear in acrobatic tights. It is, I guarantee, a sight for sore eyes. In fact, several oculists have booked blocks of seats for their patients at the first sneak preview. The other great moment occurs when I render "Lydia the Tattooed Lady" in my boyish tenor. Speaking of boyish tenors, Kenny Baker has a small part in our epic and is a slight improvement over Allan Jones. The fellow was constantly dogging my footsteps asking for singing advice and the secrets of my—"

"The reason that Jane and I are going to Manhattan is because they want to turn *Hollywood Molly* into a radio show."

"Would you like me to sing a bit of 'Lydia the Tattooed Lady'?"

"No."

"I take that as a negative response, meaning you don't wish to enjoy an experience that's been compared with seeing Caruso in his prime? Of course, seeing Caruso in his underwear was an equally fascinating experience and I consider myself fortunate to have witnessed—"

"You sang the entire song for me the last time we had lunch," I reminded him.

"Great songs bear repeating. I wager you've heard 'The Star Spangled Banner' more than once."

"The what?"

Mellman returned and put a fresh cup of coffee before Groucho. "We're all out of hemlock," he said and went away.

Groucho located his cigar again, lit it, and leaned back in the booth. "Are you kiddies flying to New York, Rollo?"

"Nope, taking the Super Chief. Jane's uneasy about airplanes so—"

"A pity and a shame, young man, because I'm flying to Manhattan early next week," Groucho informed me. "We could have shared a plane and I might've obtained the services of my old chum Crash Corrigan to pilot it for us. Some folks don't like to fly with Crash, because of his unfortunate first name, but I for one—"

"Why are you going to New York?" I managed to ask.

"Not, as you might suspect, to get away from the scene of our recent crime at MGM," he assured me. "Actually, I've been invited to appear in a streamlined version of *The Mikado*. They're planning for a limited run on Broadway and possibly a series of previews at the New York World's Fair."

"You're playing who?"

"They want me to be the Lord High Executioner. I would've preferred being the Three Little Maids from School, but this Ko-Ko part isn't bad either. Perhaps you're aware of my fondness for Gilbert and Sullivan."

"I knew you were that way about Sullivan, but who's this Gilbert guy?"

"Not a great exit line," he observed, sliding free of the booth and heading for the cashier. "But I intend, sirrah, to utilize it as such."

When we emerged onto the sunny afternoon sidewalk, two amply built dark-haired young men in wide-shouldered pinstripe suits were waiting for us.

Two

The larger and wider of the two hoods discreetly slipped his hand inside his jacket to pat what was no doubt a shoulder holster. "Mr. Marx, would you and your colleague like to come with us to pay a little visit to Vince Salermo?"

"What a shame, because normally we'd both jump at the chance to drop in on one of the most respected gangsters in all of southern California," answered Groucho apologetically. "However, we just bought a lifetime supply of trolley tokens and took a vow never to ride with strange men until we use them all—"

"The boss said to inform you that this is a courteous invitation, Mr. Marx, and you are free to accompany us or not."

The second hoodlum added, "And we're not to hurt you *seriously* if you refuse."

We decided to go for a ride.

Maybe it was the heat of the afternoon, but I found myself perspiring somewhat profusely as we were escorted, much too politely, to an extremely long black limousine that was illegally parked beneath a palm tree just around the corner.

There was an extremely pretty perfumed blonde already seated in the shadowy backseat when we climbed in.

"Aren't you Groucho Marx?" she asked, her black satiny dress whispering as she slid to the far side of the wide seat.

"Which one of us are you addressing that query to, my dear?" asked Groucho as he plumped down close beside her.

"You, Mr. Marx."

"Just as well, because if you were asking Frank here, he'd have grounds for a substantial lawsuit for slander. He'd also have grounds for an attractive off-the-shoulder sunsuit with enough material left over to upholster his love seat."

Giggling, she produced an autograph album from her black-leather purse. "I collect signatures."

"Well, the only one I have on my person at the moment is that of John Quincy Shapiro. He was supposed to be one of the original signers of the Declaration of Independence, but he got there too late and ended up having to sign the caterer's bill instead."

"No. What I want is *your* signature." Opening the book to a blank page, she plopped it down on his lap.

Our two escorts had settled into the front seat, with the larger at the wheel. The big car came quietly to life and moved away from the curb.

"And what's your name, my child?"

"Bubbles."

"I'll refrain from commenting on that in any way." He gazed, thoughtfully, out at the streets of Hollywood that we were speeding through. We passed a large, high billboard advertising *Beau Geste,* Paramount's new Foreign Legion epic. Groucho frowned in its direction, then scrawled something and returned the autograph album to the pretty blonde.

Nearsighted apparently, Bubbles brought the page up close to her eye-shadowed eyes. " 'Best wishes, Groucho Marx,' " she read aloud, sounding a bit disappointed. "Gee, that's not especially witty."

"Alas, kiddo," he said, "I'm never at my wittiest when I'm in the process of being dragooned and kidnapped."

"Hey," said the smaller hoodlum, glowering back at us. "Don't talk like that, Mr. Marx. This is just a friendly little drive."

Groucho sighed. "Oh, forgive me for being such a silly goose," he said. "But even a *friendly* kidnapping gives me the heebie-jeebies."

We were driven to a hoping-to-be fashionable new Italian restaurant just off La Cienega. Its name, emblazoned in white script on the blue awning out front, was Fior d'Italia. The long dark car parked in the small, nearly empty lot behind the place.

Bubbles remained in the backseat. "I hope I meet you again when you're in a better mood, Mr. Marx," she called as we were led toward the restaurant.

"If I'd been in a better mood," he called back, "I'd probably have assaulted you. So count your blessings. You might, in fact, also count the silverware, since I suspect—"

"It's not a very good idea," suggested the larger gangster, "to flirt with the boss's current fiancée."

"Well, send around a few of his former fiancées then and I'll charm them."

Another large man in a dark suit opened the restaurant's rear door from the inside, glared out, and eyed our group. "Okay," he said, giving a come-in nod of his head.

We were ushered along a narrow hallway and into a large, brand-new kitchen.

Vince Salermo himself, decked out in a striped apron and a fluffy chef's hat, was squatting near one of the ovens, studying a baking dish that held lasagna. Salermo was a small, compact man in his early fifties, deeply tanned and a shade taller than five foot four. He stood up and smiled at us.

Lounging around the kitchen were three other large young men in suits, all of whom gave the impression that they were armed.

"Good to see you, Groucho, Frank," said Salermo as he carefully shut the oven.

"Does the health department know your kitchen is infested with goniffs?" inquired Groucho.

The small gangster scowled, removing his high white hat. "Hey, I don't mind a little good-natured kidding, Groucho, but—"

"I assure you, Vincent, that I'm always extremely good-natured with anybody wearing anything that remotely resembles a concealed weapon," Groucho told him, parking on a stool next to a chopping block.

The kitchen smelled strongly of herbs like rosemary and oregano, with an overlay of aftershave lotion and hair tonic.

Salermo, who was the head of Mob gambling in southern California, nodded at one of his men. "Untie this damn thing," he said, indicating his apron.

"I was just mentioning to Frank today," said Groucho while a young hoodlum helped Salermo free of the apron, "how much we like conundrums and puzzles and riddles. But, Vincent, rather than letting us figure it out ourselves, suppose you tell us why the hell you grabbed us off a peaceful Beverly Hills street and dragged us into this culinary sinkhole?"

Salermo gestured to another of his men and was handed a copy of the *Los Angeles Times*. "This is why," he said, angry, pointing at the front-page story about the shooting of Nick Sanantonio.

"One of your boys, wasn't he?" asked Groucho, plucking a sliver of bell pepper off the chopping counter.

"Yeah, Nick was one of my most prized lieutenants, you might say." He slapped, backhanded, at the newspaper columns. "This rag says he was gunned down this morning when he left his Brentwood mansion to take a short walk. Why that bastard wanted to walk when he's got three cars, I don't know."

"As I understand it, there were a couple of witnesses," said Groucho. "They say a black car came roaring by and somebody felled your boy with a shotgun blast. Sounds pretty much like a typical—"

"We'll come to that, Groucho," cut in the gangster. "The thing is, you and Denby here have been doing pretty good catching killers."

"We're semiretired," Groucho assured him. "Fact is, I'm thinking of opening up a snake farm near Palm Springs and Frank—"

"Let me finish, huh?" Salermo moved closer to Groucho. "The papers and the assholes on the radio are saying this was a gang killing. But it wasn't at all."

"Black car, shotgun," reminded Groucho. "Those are all the standard props for a traditional—"

"Listen, Groucho, I didn't have Nick rubbed out and, trust me, neither did any of our rivals."

Groucho took out a fresh cigar and slowly unwrapped it. "Meaning what?"

"Nick Sanantonio was killed for some other reason altogether."

"Any ideas what that reason was?"

"No. Which is where you two guys come in," answered Salermo. "See, I know damned well this was some kind of private murder and whoever did it worked real hard to make it look like a gang killing."

"Tell the police about it, Vincent, and—"

"I'm not in a position at the moment to discuss my theory with the cops," cut in the gangster. "However, Groucho, I'm willing to pay you and Denby a fee of, say, five thousand bucks to work on the case. With a bonus if you find out who killed the poor guy and why."

Biting down on his cigar, Groucho gave a shake of his head. "The way you state your case, Vincent, it sounds as though solving this mystery is almost our civic duty," he said. "But, alas, my partner and I are, for separate reasons, shortly going to be departing for far-distant New York City. In which mecca we'll be staying for an untold period of time. Therefore, much as we'd adore it, we can't possibly work on this particular—"

"Postpone your trip," Salermo told him.

"These are business deals," I said. "In my case, my wife and I have to be in Manhattan to—"

"How about you, Groucho?"

"I've signed a contract to tread the boards and warble," he answered. "Such a legal document is inviolate. Besides coming in violet, it can also be ordered in several other fashionable shades for your fall wardrobe."

"He's razzing you, boss," complained one of the attendant hoods.

"Aw, that's just his way," said Salermo, though not looking especially pleased. He took two slow breaths, in and out. "I've got to tell you, Groucho, that I'm pretty damned disappointed."

"You might try Philip Marlowe, Dan Turner, or some other Hollywood shamus," suggested Groucho helpfully. "Admittedly, they don't have our track record, our sterling reputation, or a strawberry birthmark right here, and yet—"

"Tell you what," cut in the gangster. "If this mess hasn't been cleared up by the time you guys get back, I'll maybe send some of my boys to fetch you again."

"I've been thinking of settling down permanently on a farm in Bucks County, Pennsylvania," Groucho said. "Or possibly in nearby Ducks County, which is very like Bucks County except it has feathers. However, if I ever do return to Hollywood and vicinity, do give me a buzz. Or you might give me a big box of saltwater taffy, which—"

"Rudy, you and Archie run our guests back to where you found them," Salermo ordered the guy who'd driven us over.

"Nice seeing you and yours once again." Groucho was about to light his cigar, when he paused and sniffed at the kitchen air. "I think your lasagna's burning."

When we were back in front of Moonbaum's deli, Groucho took a polka-dot handkerchief out of his trouser pocket and wiped his brow. "To paraphrase Napoleon after the Battle of Waterloo," he observed, *"oy gevalt."*

Three

I got home to our beach cottage in the town of Bayside just ahead of twilight. The day was starting to fade and the nearby Pacific Ocean was already turning paler. A gaggle of seagulls was circling overhead, squawking forlornly to each other.

Jane was in the living room, surrounded by what I judged to be too many suitcases to take to New York with us. She was having a serious conversation with our dog.

Dorgan, a bloodhound and a retired movie dog, had been Groucho's present to us the past Christmas.

"We'll only be away for about ten days, Dorgan," she was explaining, kneeling beside him and rubbing his stomach. "Elena Sederholm is an old art school chum of mine and she and her husband really like dogs."

Dorgan tilted his head in my direction and let his tongue loll out by way of greeting.

"You've probably heard me talk about how absolutely dull the Sederholms are," Jane continued to the dog. "But that's only from a human perspective, keep in mind. They're not likely to ask *you* to play whist and, when it comes down to it, almost anybody can rub your tummy and—"

"Not with your deft touch," I put in.

15

"Hey, don't go saying that in front of him." Jane stood up, smoothing down her skirt. "Welcome home, by the way. How come you look so frazzled?"

After persuading Dorgan not to keep jumping at my groin, I kissed my wife. "Well, it's mostly because Groucho and I had sort of an impromptu business meeting with Vince Salermo."

"Salermo? Wasn't he the one who bopped you on the sconce and had you shanghaied to his gambling ship while you and Groucho were working on Peg McMorrow's murder?"

"That's the Vince Salermo I'm alluding to, yeah."

She gave an unhappy shake of her head. "My God, they might've shot you. Those fellas are always going around mowing each other down," she said, upset. "Just today they bumped off Nick Sanantonio."

"So I've heard," I said, putting my hands on her slim shoulders. "Fact is, hon, that's why Salermo had us transported from out in front of Moonbaum's to his—"

"Those goons took you and Groucho for a ride?"

"In a way, sort of," I replied and recounted to her what had taken place in the kitchen at the Fior d'Italia.

At the conclusion of my explanation, Jane took a step back. "Well, okay, but what about the movie actress?"

"Eh?" I inquired, cupping my hand to my ear. "I don't recall including a movie actress in my scenario. What are you talking about, Jane?"

"I was listening to Johnny Whistler's Hollywood gossip broadcast while I was at the drawing board this afternoon," she said. "By the way, he says he's heard Groucho's new movie isn't up to snuff."

"The actress?"

"Whistler asked one of those questions of his." She paused to recall the exact wording. " 'What major movie studio is working night and day to hush up the rumors that one of its big cinemactresses had a recent hot-time affair with the notorious Nick Sanantonio, the handsome gangland figure who was gunned down like a dog in fashionable Brentwood early today?' Or words to that effect."

"Listening to Johnny Whistler too much is going to stunt your vocabulary."

"Okay, but who's the actress? What did Salermo tell you guys?"

I shook my head. "He didn't mention any movie stars at all, or even a starlet or a dress extra."

"Sanantonio was supposed to be quite a ladies' man."

"Even so, the subject didn't come up while we were chatting with his boss."

"I wonder who it is."

Dorgan made a bored noise, waddled toward our sofa, hoisted himself up onto it. He sprawled, shutting his eyes.

"Hey, you're not," I mentioned to him, "supposed to sit up there."

"It's okay," said Jane, putting her hand on my arm. "I gave him permission, because he's been so droopy about my packing to go on this trip."

"Speaking of trips," I said, settling into an armchair, "it turns out that Groucho's going to New York, too."

She made a surprised inhaling noise. "Not with us?"

I pointed at the ceiling. "Flying."

Eyeing me, she asked, "And you're certain you two aren't planning to go into the detective business in Manhattan?"

"Nope, we have no such plans, ma'am," I assured my wife. "He's going back there to do some solo work, without his brothers. On Broadway and probably also at the New York World's Fair."

"He's not going to take over for Johnny Weismuller in Billy Rose's Aquacade?"

"Actually, he's going to be starring in a streamlined version of *The Mikado*."

She was crouching by the suitcases. "Do you think we can fit seven pieces of baggage in our compartment on the Super Chief?"

"All of that's *your* luggage, and I counted eight pieces."

"Eventually I'll narrow mine down to five."

"Leaving me two?"

She stood up. "*The Mikado,* huh?"

"Groucho's pretty good at singing that stuff."

"He's somewhat better than Gene Autry would be," Jane conceded. "And about equal to Wee Bonnie Baker."

"He sang at our wedding," I reminded.

"But not selections from Gilbert and Sullivan."

I stretched up out of my chair. "Want to go out to dinner?"

"Not tonight. I still have to finish up that promotion drawing to take back east with us," she answered, rising to her feet and heading toward her studio. "Can you give me a quick opinion of something?"

"Sure, and at no extra cost." Dorgan and I followed her.

Tacked side by side on the drawing board were two pencilled drawings of the main characters in *Hollywood Molly.* "Which one do you think works best?" she asked me.

In the left hand one, her comic strip characters were gathered around a Beverly Hills–style swimming pool. The other drawing showed them on a sound stage, where some sort of nightclub sequence was being shot.

"Swimming pool has more sex appeal," I said. "But the other one gives more of a feel of Hollywood and the movies."

"Do you think B. P. Obelisk looks too pudgy in that pair of swimming trunks?"

B. P. Obelisk was the head of the movie studio Molly worked for, Pyramid Pictures. Among the others gathered around him and Molly at the poolside were her director, Leroy Panorama, Jr., her cowboy actor boyfriend, Sam Wyoming, her actress pal, Vicky Fairweather, and her cat, Boswell.

Jane said, "I'm wondering if the advertising people and the radio executives won't be more impressed with the bathing suit approach."

"No doubt they will," I agreed, "but you've had flap from your newspaper syndicate before when Molly looked, and I quote, 'too provocative.' "

"You think that two-piece bathing suit is too provocative?"

"Not me, my love, but then I don't work for the Empire Feature Syndicate of Manhattan."

"You're probably right. Best to play it safe."

"Or you might do them both."

"It'll take too much time to ink both, so I'll settle for the studio shot." She pointed at the black-and-white cat. "I've been redesigning Boswell. Does he look like anybody you know?"

"He appears to be sporting the feline equivalent of a Groucho moustache."

"Yep. I was tempted to add a cigar, too, but decided that would probably be too provocative."

"Oh, and speaking of Groucho—he invited us to dine with him while we're in New York," I said. "As long as—"

"—we go Dutch on the check."

"As long as we go Dutch on the check," I confirmed.

Four

The El Perro Lindo restaurant was on Olvera Street in Los Angeles, a short walk from the recently inaugurated Union Station over on Alameda Boulevard. Early Friday night, after checking our luggage, Jane and I dropped in there for dinner. The Santa Fe Super Chief was due to depart for points east at eight o'clock.

"Six isn't bad," Jane was saying across our table.

"Better than nine."

She had been able, after considerable note taking, soul-searching, unpacking, and repacking, to narrow her number of suitcases to four. "I think it's admirable," she said, picking up her menu, "the sacrifices I made in my wardrobe. I was planning to stun the syndicate executives and all the radio people with the infinite variety of my clothes. But now . . ." She shrugged.

"You're innately stunning," I assured her. "You don't need all those extra dresses and—"

"Just because you only have two suits to your name is no reason to—"

"I epitomize the casual California approach. It's sports coats, polo shirts, and slacks that the fashionable male wears in these parts."

She studied the menu for a moment. "I think I'll try the *chiles rel-*

21

lenos," she decided. "Maybe you'll be lucky and lose that pumpkin-colored sports coat of yours on the trip."

"That particular coat has been favorably commented on by several arbiters of fashion."

"It looks like something Groucho would wear."

"Well, as a matter of fact, Groucho was one of the fashion arbiters who said nice things about it."

The Mexican restaurant was of medium size, with about a dozen white-clothed tables around the main dining room. The low-volume jukebox specialized in tunes by Tito Guizar. There was a cocktail bar near the entrance and through the high, wide front window you could see the brick-paved courtyard, part of a decorative fountain, and a collection of potted cactus. Dusk was just beginning to settle in and lights were coming on outside.

About half the surrounding tables were occupied so far.

"That's interesting," I observed, after glancing around the place.

"What is?"

"At that table over near the little stage," I answered. "That's Willa Jerome."

Casually, Jane turned to take a look. "The studiously plain one with the glasses?"

"Nope, the gorgeous one with the pale complexion, blonde hair, and patrician look."

"She's the one Twentieth Century Fox signed, with much hoopla, last year, isn't she?"

"Yeah, she was supposedly already a movie star over in her native England. Twentieth imported her and stuck her into *Trafalgar Square* with Tyrone Power. It's supposed to open next week."

"Going to be boffo at the box office," commented my wife. "Or so Johnny Whistler predicted the other day."

"I'd say more socko than boffo."

"Who's the portly gent with them?"

"No idea." There was a chubby blonde guy of about forty at the table

22

with the two women. He had on a very businesslike grey suit and his puffy face was flushed. Three empty Dos Equis beer bottles stood next to his plate.

Jane said, "Maybe Willa Jerome is the one."

"The one what?"

"Who had the torrid affair with the late Nick Sanantonio."

"You'll have to stay tuned to Johnny Whistler to find out."

Our waiter appeared and inquired, "Have you and the señora decided, señor?"

"My wife'll have the *rellenos* and I'll try the number three combination."

"And to drink?"

I looked across at Jane and she shook her head. "Just water for now."

"Bueno," he said and left us.

"Several people," Jane said, "have asked me if this trip of ours is going to be a second—"

"Frank," said a raspy voice, "what the hell are you doing in this joint?"

"Getting ready to embark on a second honeymoon on the Super Chief," I said to the tall, lean man who'd come over to our table. It was Larry Shell, a *Los Angeles Times* photographer.

He had his camera dangling in his left hand. "I just popped in for a beer and spotted you and . . . this is your wife, isn't it?"

"We're pretending I am," said Jane, smiling sweetly up at him. "There's some kind of law against transporting unmarried women across state lines for dubious purposes."

"This is my wife," I said. "Jane Danner, Larry Shell."

"Hey, that's a great comic strip you do, Janey," said the photographer. "I read *Hollywood Molly* every damn day faithfully. Except Tuesdays, when I'm usually too hungover to read much of anything."

"I can send you a synopsis every Tuesday," she offered.

"You on your way to Union Station?" I asked him.

"Yeah, monumental events are unfolding there and I've got to get some pictures. Supposed to meet Bockman over there. He's going to do the story."

"What story?" asked Jane. "Not a train wreck?"

"Nope, nothing so interesting," answered Shell. "It's Daniel K. Manheim, the man who would be David O. Selznick. He thinks he's got another Vivien Leigh in the person of some skinny broad he's calling Dian Bowers."

"She's the one Manheim's starring in his million-buck movie production of *Saint Joan,* huh?" I said.

"The same, yeah," answered Shell. "Me, I'd title the flicker *Manheim's Folly,* but certain powers at the god damn paper are convinced that the fact that Manheim and Miss Bowers are leaving tonight for New York City, where he intends to premiere the flicker, introduce her to his money people and the press, is a big event." He patted his camera. "So I've got to take some immortal pics."

"We'll see you over there," I said.

He leaned, patted Jane on the back. "Bon voyage, Janey," he said and headed off.

I watched him step out into the deepening twilight. "Larry's something of a jerk," I explained. "But he's a good photographer."

Jane waited until our waiter had delivered two glasses of water, then said, "So we're going to have Dian Bowers and her Svengali on our journey East."

"Sounds like it. And probably Willa Jerome and her entourage."

"Maybe we ought to wait for the next circus train. It'll probably be quieter."

I was looking over toward the bar. "And there's another potential fellow traveler."

"The fella who looks like a football player who's gone to seed?"

Nodding, I answered, "He actually used to be a football player at USC about ten years back. That's Hal Arneson."

"He's Manheim's publicity flack now, isn't he?"

"Publicity man, bodyguard, troubleshooter," I said. "All-around handyman at Manheim Productions, Inc."

"Oops, he's rising up from his stool and heading this way. Is he another friend of yours?"

"No, Arneson and I aren't close. He's not coming to chat with us."

The large blonde man walked by our table, with a quick nod at me, and crossed to that of Willa Jerome. He was wearing a rumpled blue suit and a hand-painted tie that showed a sunset over a tropical isle.

Smiling, Willa stood up and exchanged hugs with the publicity man. "Hal, darling," she said in her drawling British accent. "So wonderful to see you. Are you going to be taking the Super Chief?"

"Right, kid. I'm tagging along with Manheim and Dian Bowers."

"I've heard the girl is marvelous," said Willa.

"That's putting it mildly," said Arneson, grinning.

Five

Hand in hand, Jane and I approached Union Station through the oncoming night. It glowed up ahead of us, a large, sprawling structure of tinted stucco and red-tile roofs, dominated by a clock tower. Built at the cost of over ten million bucks, it looked like the result of an uneasy collaboration between Father Junipero Serra and Cecil B. DeMille.

The pillared art deco lamps out front were on, lending a Hollywood glow to the sidewalk and the decorative palm trees along Alameda Boulevard. As we approached the entrance to the vast waiting room, two yellow cabs pulled up to the curb. A half-dozen or so buoyant young people came bouncing out, laughing, chattering, and unloading an assortment of suitcases. Two Red Cap porters hurried over with luggage carts. From out of the trunk of the rear cab the driver tugged a battered trunk that had "STEP RIGHT UP" freshly lettered on the side in whitewash.

"Pretty girls," I mentioned.

"Pretty boys, too," said Jane.

"Dancers, maybe?"

"Yep. *Step Right Up* is a new musical that's trying out in Chicago before, maybe, opening on Broadway," said Jane. "With a cast of Hollywood hopefuls."

"More information obtained from Johnny Whistler?"

"Louella Parsons in this case." We entered the vast, high-ceilinged waiting room. "Bear in mind, dear, that I have to keep up-to-date with goings-on in movie land. Background stuff for *Hollywood Molly*. It's not that I'm addicted to show business gossip."

"I'm a Hollywood hopeful myself at the moment," I mentioned. "If only I could dance better, I might join this show."

"First thing to do is improve your fox trot, then work up from there."

The waiting room still had a brand-new smell to it. You got the feeling you'd entered a huge, new, and affluent Beverly Hills church and that the rows of leather settees were pews. The high-hanging chandeliers were made of gold-tinted glass and added a soft, expensive glow to everything.

Midway into the big vaulted room, at the edge of the pastel-tiled walkway leading to the access tunnel for the train platforms, was gathered a small crowd of people. Reporters, photographers, curious passengers. I spotted Larry Shell, using his camera, and Dan Bockman from the *LA Times*. Also Norm Lenzer of the *Herald-Examiner*, Gil Lumbard of the *Hollywood Citizen-News,* a fat guy who worked, I think, for the *San Diego Union,* and an attractive blonde I was pretty sure was Sheilah Graham. They were all circling a smiling Daniel K. Manheim and an obviously nervous Dian Bowers. The producer was a large, heavyset man in his early forties, his thick wavy hair already a silvery white. He was wearing a well-tailored—all things considered—dark grey suit and had his right arm protectively around the slim shoulders of the slim, dark-haired young actress. She was pretty, but not in a glamour-girl way, and her hair was still worn in the short cropped style that portraying Joan of Arc had called for. Standing nearby, in a soldier-at-ease position, was the burly Hal Arneson.

"Want to stop and listen?" I asked Jane.

She shrugged her left shoulder. "Might as well. We've still got about twenty minutes before the train starts."

". . . weren't you in the movies before, Dian?" Lenzer was asking.

"Norm, Miss Bowers is a brand-new, freshly minted motion picture star," Manheim answered for her in his deep chesty voice. "As bright and new as this railway station. *Saint Joan,* which will have its world premiere in New York City late next week, is Dian Bowers's very first movie. I'm very proud of this new discovery of mine and, I might add, we've just heard that the author of *Saint Joan,* none other than George Bernard Shaw himself, has just viewed a rough cut of the film, which we rushed to him in England. The word is that GBS is raving about it."

Lumbard said, "They say he's not only raving, he's screaming, yelling, and threatening to sic his pack of lawyers on you, Manheim."

"This is no place for making jokes, Gil," the hefty producer told him. "Dian's performance in my production of *Saint Joan* is—"

"I know I saw you in B Westerns, honey," persisted Lenzer, pushing closer to the uneasy actress.

"No, you must be mistaken, Mr. Lenzer," Dian replied softly. "As Mr. Manheim has explained, this is my very first film and—"

"Who'd believe that son of a bitch?" asked a lean young man who'd just come up to the edge of the group surrounding the producer and his protégée.

"One of the dancers," whispered Jane.

"Not too smart for a Hollywood hopeful to malign Manheim," I whispered back. "Even if he is a little soused."

"Young man, you're interrupting," said Manheim evenly.

Ignoring him, the young dancer said to the reporters, "Why don't you ask him about Kathy Sutter?" His voice was too loud, and had a blurred edge to it. "See what he has to say about *her.*"

Hal Arneson had worked his way over to him. "What say, sonny, you lay off the heckling?" He took hold of his upper arm, tightly.

"What say you take a flying leap at the moon, you god damn Gestapo." He started to swing at the big troubleshooter.

Arneson grinned, dodged, and caught the fist. He used the arm as a lever to turn the angry dancer around. "You keep acting up, kid, and the station cops are going to haul you away," he warned. "Calm down, huh, and go catch your train."

29

"C'mon, Len, let's get aboard." A platinum blonde, not more than nineteen, caught the young guy's hand. "Better take it easy."

"But that bastard . . ." He didn't finish the sentence, shook his head instead. Scowling, he jerked free of Arneson's grasp. "Okay, all right. For now." He let the blonde dancer lead him away.

As Jane and I continued on our way, she said, "Intrigue always enlivens a train trip."

I was glancing around the big waiting room, scanning the place. "Um," I muttered.

"What's the matter, Frank?"

"Nothing," I replied. "It's only that I thought maybe Groucho would be here to see us off."

"Did he say he would?"

"Nope, not exactly," I admitted. "But he asked a lot of questions about which train we were taking, and when it was leaving." I glanced around again. "I guess he's not here, though."

"Count your blessings," she advised.

The Santa Fe Super Chief was an impressively streamlined diesel train. It consisted of nine gleaming stainless-steel cars and its sharp-nosed engine, which was painted a bright red and gold in a design that was supposed to suggest an Indian war bonnet. Just sitting there on the tracks beside the night platform, the train gave the impression it was surging ahead.

"Nice design," I commented as we headed back in the direction of our train car.

Jane said, "Doesn't Buck Rogers fly around in something that looks a lot like our engine?"

"You're thinking of Flash Gordon."

Up ahead of us some fifteen feet or so Willa Jerome and the two people we'd seen having dinner with her were walking. The chubby blonde man was seriously unstable on his feet and kept swaying into the actress.

"Honestly, Phil," Willa said, frowning and giving him a small shove. "Try and stay upright at least until we reach our drawing room, can't you?"

"Sorry, my pet." He was carrying what looked like a medical bag and as he stumbled away from her side, it became entangled with his legs. "Oops."

The plain young woman in glasses reached out to catch him, but he fell over and landed, hard, on the platform.

He let go of the black bag, which hit the planks with a rattling thunk.

Sprinting forward, I bent beside the sprawled man. "You okay?"

"Perfectly fine and in ship shape," he assured me in a boozy murmur. "I simply completely and totally lost the ability to navigate. Nothing serious."

I took hold of his arm. "C'mon, I'll help you up."

"That's very Good Samaritan of you, old man," he said, exhaling a breath that was strongly scented with the odor of Mexican beer and stale bourbon.

After some grunting and creaking on his part, we got him into a standing position.

The young woman, who I figured must be Willa's secretary, said to me, "Thank you very much. Dr. Dowling's getting over a bout of influenza and he's wobbly."

"Four beers didn't help much either," added Willa, who was watching us, frowning, arms folded.

"Three beers," the plump doctor corrected. "And thank you, sir. I'm in your debt."

"All part of our friendly service," I said.

"If you have a headache during our trip East or find yourself in the need of minor surgery, give a holler," said Dr. Dowling, brushing at his suit.

"You'd be better off calling Dr. Kildare." Willa snatched his black bag up off the platform and thrust it at him. "Let's move along, Philip."

She turned on her heel and started off. The tipsy doctor, after taking a deep breath, went wobbling along after her.

The secretary said, "Thank you again," and hurried away in their wake.

Jane said, "That must be Philip Dowling."

"That was the name that was bandied about, yeah."

"He's Willa Jerome's personal physician. Travels with her, holds her hand between scenes on the set," she said. "Must be nice to have a personal physician."

"I'm happier with a personal cartoonist," I said, taking her hand again. "Here's the car we're looking for."

A porter was waiting for us just outside Compartment F. "Good evening, folks. I'm Earl Johnson and I'll be looking after you on your Super Chief trip to Chicago. And I'll see that you change trains for New York," he explained. "The journey to Chicago takes exactly thirty-nine-and-a-half hours, give or take a half hour."

"My husband needs all the looking after he can get," said Jane. "Did our luggage get here?"

"Yes, ma'am. I took care of that myself," Johnson answered. "First call for dinner is at eight-thirty. You want me to put you down for—"

"We already ate, thanks." I handed him four bits. "That'll do for now."

"Welcome aboard, folks," he said and moved along the corridor.

"Want me to carry you across the threshold?" I asked Jane.

"Not necessary." She stepped into our compartment.

I followed and slid the door shut behind us. "Roomy."

"And Venetian blinds on the windows."

"For an extra thirty-nine bucks, they'd better include Venetian blinds."

"Hey, my newspaper syndicate is paying for all this, remember?"

"Are you implying that I can't afford to keep my wife in Venetian blinds?"

Smiling, she came over and hugged me. "Let's pretend we won this trip playing Bingo. Then you won't feel like a kept man. Okay?"

"If I were a kept man, we'd be traveling in a drawing room." I kissed her.

The streamlined Super Chief glided out of Union Station at about ten minutes after eight. Nighttime Los Angeles rapidly grew up all around us, our view sliced by the Venetian blinds.

Out in the corridor a steward went by, striking that sort of miniature glockenspiel they carry, and announcing, "First call to dinner. First call to dinner."

Jane had taken her shoes off and was sitting on our narrow stream-lined reddish-brown couch, her legs tucked under her. "Can I confess something?"

"So long as it doesn't involve any criminal activities you were involved in before our marriage."

"It's just that I'm kind of anxious about this trip to New York," she admitted. "The business side of things, I mean. I've never met most of those syndicate executives before, not to mention the network people."

"You'll charm them, Jane," I assured her. "And the ones you can't charm, I'll take care of."

"I guess you're right. Together, we can charm the birds down out of the trees."

"Which could result in a lot of birds underfoot," I said. "Want to find the club car and have a drink?"

"Not a drink, no," she said, standing up. "But a cup of coffee maybe."

Soon as she located both her shoes and put them on, we moved out into the corridor of the gently swaying car.

Our porter was standing nearby. "Help you folks?"

"Club car is which way?" I asked.

"It's called the cocktail lounge, sir." Johnson pointed forward. "Go through this car, then the dining car, and it'll be on the other side of that."

The dining car, judging by the number of tables, would accommodate about three dozen. But there were only about fifteen passengers scattered around it so far. Sharing a table were the young dancer who'd interrupted Manheim and the platinum blonde who'd persuaded him to move along. He appeared to be somewhat less angry.

The door at the other end of the car opened and a middle-aged couple came in. Some music from the cocktail lounge drifted in with them.

"That's Groucho singing," realized Jane. "But I don't recognize the song."

"It's called 'Lydia the Tattooed Lady,' " I said, frowning. "Harold Arlen and Yip Harburg wrote it for *At the Circus*. But I didn't know Groucho had already made a record of it."

Jane shook her head. "That's no phonograph record, ninny," she told me. "That's got to be Groucho himself."

And it was.

Six

We found Groucho perched on the arm of one of the brownish chairs along the wall of the lounge. Wearing an ochre-colored sports coat, an olive green polo shirt, and slacks of a shade I'd never seen before, he was strumming his steel-string guitar and finishing up "Lydia the Tattooed Lady."

Circled close around his chair were four of the girl dancers from *Step Right Up*, plus three other female passengers.

When Groucho finished the song and tagged it with a few flamenco flourishes on the guitar, the surrounding girls applauded and made appreciative noises.

Several of the other passengers in the moving cocktail lounge clapped as well. A plump matron seated near the bar with her plump husband started to reach into her purse.

From his chair across from Groucho, Hal Arneson, the husky troubleshooter with the tropical sunset necktie, made a mock toasting gesture with his nearly empty highball glass. "Too bad you aren't as funny as you think you are, Groucho," he called.

"Nobody is," Groucho answered.

"I think he's colossal," said a pretty blonde dancer, wrinkling her nose at Arneson.

"Actually a recent exhaustive study conducted by the Harvard Business School determined that I was *super*colossal, my dear," corrected

Groucho as he dropped his guitar into its scuffed case and then raised his left eyebrow in the direction of a pretty redhead. "And what did *you* think of my performance, miss?"

"Very impressive,"

"Why, thank you."

"Yeah, very impressive the way you can strum your guitar and pinch my fanny at the same time."

"Merely a little trick I picked up from my old chum Segovia."

A pretty brunette asked, "You know Andrés Segovia, the world-famous guitarist?"

"No, this is Irwin Segovia, the world-famous fanny pincher." Groucho shut the guitar case and stood up.

One of the male dancers joined the group, a bottle of beer in his right hand. "The word around LA is that *At the Circus* is a turkey," he remarked.

Nodding, Groucho said, "Yes, young man, but you'll be delighted to learn that it's a *kosher* turkey. Meaning that masochists of every denomination can attend without fear of—"

"How come the Marx Brothers never make a picture in color?" asked another pretty girl.

Groucho, looking perplexed, touched his cheek. "We don't?" he asked. "No wonder I looked so pale in the rushes. Of course, you should have seen me in the bulrushes. Cute as a bug's ear I was when they plucked me out of the stream and—"

"C'mon, what's the real reason you guys never appear in Technicolor?"

Sighing, Groucho raised his eyes toward the sand-colored domed ceiling. "It's a sad story, young lady," he replied. "It all has to do with Natalie Kalmus, the statuesque beauty who controls Technicolor—and when I say statuesque, I'm alluding to that statue of General Grant in the local park. At any rate, Natalie has never forgiven me because of an unfortunate incident in a phone booth in Tijuana. She—"

"You told us a little while ago, Groucho, that you were in that phone booth with Joan Crawford."

"I was, when who should walk by but Natalie Kalmus. It made quite a scene, especially in Technicolor."

The plump woman had made her way to the edge of the group now, autograph album in hand. She said, "I just love you in the movies, Mr. Marx."

"How about loving me in the baggage car—say in about an hour?"

The plump husband popped to his feet. "Here now, you can't talk to my wife that way."

"I most certainly can, sir. I have a valid permit from the Fish and Game . . . ah, do my old eyes deceive me or is that Frank Denby and the lovely Jane Danner I see yonder?" He hopped down from his chair and started slouching his way toward us.

"Who the hell is Frank Denby?" asked one of the male dancers.

"Don't know. Nobody famous. But Jane Danner draws that great comic strip."

Groucho took hold of Jane's hand and, bowing low and with considerable sound effects, kissed it several times.

"How come you're on the Super Chief?" I asked him as he straightened up.

He curtsied to me and explained, "I was feeling extremely avuncular yesterday, Rollo. It therefore occurred to me that you two innocents needed someone older and wiser to chaperone you on this perilous journey across uncharted lands. I couldn't think of anyone who filled the bill, so I decided to tag along myself. At great personal expense and admirable sacrifice, I cancelled my plane ticket and booked a compartment on this very train." He held up a cautionary finger. "I'm a mere two rooms over from you, my children, and I intend to meditate and practice my Tibetan yoga for the entire trip. So keep the caterwauling down to a minimum, if you please."

"Why, Groucho, what a wonderful surprise this is," said Jane, smiling sweetly at him. "My horoscope predicted a train disaster, but this is even better."

Jane and I sat with Groucho in the dining car while he had his dinner. As the Super Chief was pulling out of the Pomona station, a plump woman in a flowered dress came over, somewhat cautiously, to stand near our white-clothed table.

Very quietly she held out a red-covered autograph album. "I'd be honored to have your autograph, Mr. Marx," she told him.

Groucho looked up from the menu he'd been studying. "No, you wouldn't, madam. You'd be disgraced, drummed out of the corps, and run out of town on a rail," he informed her. "So remember, when you're sleeping on a park bench, that you brought it on yourself." Grabbing up a pencil from the table, he wrote in her book and returned it to her.

She studied the page, then, disappointed, said, "All this says is 'clam chowder, pot roast, and coffee.' "

"Ah, forgive me." Groucho retrieved the book. "I wrote my dinner order here by mistake." He rubbed the blunt end of the stubby pencil over his chin. "I forgot to ask you if you wanted the plain autograph or the deluxe autograph."

"What's the difference?"

"Well, the deluxe autograph involves my taking off a goodly portion of my clothes."

"I'll take the plain, please."

He wrote his name on the page beneath the prior inscription. "And now you have my permission to make a graceful exit."

The woman took her autograph book, smiled a bit tentatively at all three of us, and returned to her table. She and a thickset young guy who might have been her son were seated one table down from where Dian Bowers was sitting, somewhat uneasily, alone.

As Groucho took up the order slip, he frowned thoughtfully. "By Jove, Rollo, that young wench yonder looks deucedly familiar."

"She's Dian Bowers," I told him. "You know, Daniel Manheim's newest discovery."

"Saint Joan," added Jane.

Groucho glanced again over his shoulder at the solitary actress. "I have the distinct impression I knew her before she achieved sainthood." Concentrating on his order form, he wrote out what he wanted for dinner. "The next time I run into Fred Harvey, or any of his girls, I'm going to remind him that pastrami and lox ought to be staples on the Super Chief menu. After all, if the Donner Party had traveled with pastrami, they . . . no, her name isn't Dian Bowers."

Jane said, "Manheim probably rechristened her."

Dr. Dowling had entered the dining car from the direction of the cocktail lounge. He was less rumpled and his hair was neatly combed, but he still looked considerably wobbly on his feet.

When the train went around a slight curve in the tracks, the doctor lurched and bumped into Dian's table. "Well, good evening, Miss Bowers," he said in a blurry voice. "Mind if I join you for dinner? Of course not."

As he lowered himself into a green-backed chair, the young actress said quietly, "I'm expecting someone to join me."

"Nobody here," the doctor pointed out, gesturing vaguely at the empty chairs. "Other than us, that is. So we can have a pleasant tête-à-tête until—"

"Really, no. I'm afraid that would only cause a good deal of—"

"Nonsense, my dear. Now, if I can find the wine list, I'll order us a—"

"Miss Bowers is going to be dining with Mr. Manheim." Arneson, who'd apparently been watching from between cars, had come into the dining area and swiftly moved up behind the tipsy physician.

"It seems to me that the young lady ought to be the one who—"

"Sit elsewhere." Arneson took hold of Dr. Dowling by the coat collar and lifted him, effortlessly, clean up out of the chair.

"Well, when you put it that way." Back on his feet, Dowling tottered off, walking a weaving course through the car and out the far door.

"I'm sure Daniel will be joining you shortly, Dian." Nodding at her, Arneson withdrew from the car.

"Bless my soul," said Groucho. "I recognize her now. She had a bit part in *A Day at the Races*. Back then she was a blonde named Nancy Washburn, a struggling actress married to a struggling actor named Jim Washburn. He specialized in playing the handsome sidekick to assorted aging cowboy actors." He rose up from his seat. "I'll mosey over and say howdy."

"You're liable," warned Jane, "to get hoisted up by your collar."

"That oversized golem wouldn't risk soiling his mitts on my coat collar, kiddo."

Groucho crossed to the other side of the car and bowed to the actress. "Nice seeing you again, Nancy," he said, smiling.

She looked up, tilted her head slightly to the right. "I'm afraid you've made a mistake, Mr. Marx," she said quietly. "My name is Dian Bowers and we've never met."

Arneson had reentered the dining car and was standing, arms folded and scowling, a few feet away.

"Well, child, if you get over this bout of amnesia, I'm residing in Compartment D for the next couple days. Adios." He turned back toward our table, giving Arneson a lazy salute. "I'll save you the trouble of carrying me back to my table."

Seven

At about midnight, just as the streamliner was pulling out of the little town of Barstow and heading into the desert, someone tapped, gently, on the door of Groucho's compartment. He'd been, as he later told me, sitting there in his least threadbare bathrobe, smoking a cigar and rereading T. S. Eliot's *The Wasteland*.

"This wasteland shares several similarities with Pasadena," he said to himself. "Except Pasadena gets more rain."

At the sound of the timid knocking, Groucho rose, unlatched his door, and slid it a few inches open. "Well, fancy that," he observed. "I take it your amnesia cleared up."

It was Dian Bowers, wearing a white cablestitch sweater and tan slacks, standing there in the corridor. "Can I come in, Groucho?"

"I wouldn't want to get in trouble with the Watch and Ward Society, my dear," he said. "Or with that huge lout who plucks unwanted suitors out of your vicinity."

"Please, I'd really like to talk to you."

He opened the door wide and backed up. "My humble abode is at your service, kiddo," he invited, beckoning her with the hand that held the book.

"I didn't wake you up, did I?" the slim actress asked as she crossed the threshold.

He shut the compartment door. "Alas, I never sleep well on trains," he confided, nodding at a chair. "I never sleep well at home either, come to think of it. What causes that, I believe, is my staying awake worrying about whether or not I have insomnia."

She glanced at the book in his hand. "T. S. Eliot, huh?" she said, sitting down. "You're a lot more intellectual than you let on."

"I'd have to be." He snuffed out his cigar in a Santa Fe ashtray, settled back on his couch. "Most gorgeous movie stars who invade my sleeping chambers at this hour are consumed with lust—or they've consumed too much near beer. You, however, I sense have dropped in for some other purpose."

Dian glanced at the closed door. "I wanted to apologize, Groucho, for snubbing you in the dining car tonight."

"I'm frequently snubbed," he said. "In fact, when I was in the Boy Scouts I was only two snubs short of getting a merit badge in that category."

"I find it's easier to pretend I'm Dian Bowers and always have been. Especially when any of Daniel Manheim's people are around."

Groucho leaned forward. "Are you in some kind of trouble?"

She hesitated. "Not exactly, no," she answered after a few silent seconds. "Really, I'm in a terrific spot right now and I ought to be terribly happy and enormously grateful."

"Yet you ain't."

She said, "I don't know, Groucho. Back when I was Nancy Washburn . . . well, life was a hell of a lot simpler."

"It didn't pay as well, though."

She gave a quiet sigh. "Well, yeah, part of this is about money," the young actress admitted. "And it's also about my wanting to get someplace in this damn business. I came to Hollywood in nineteen-thirty-six, from Iola, Wisconsin, for Pete's sake. As Nancy Washburn I managed to land bit parts in exactly seven movies over the next three years."

"That averages out to over two a year."

"Sure, and I had—this is the entire total—precisely *five* lines of dialogue."

"Consider my brother Harpo. He never has any lines at all, yet he's happy as a clam," said Groucho. "Although a recent study in *Scientific American* has established that the majority of clams aren't all that happy, especially since they found out about clam chowder."

Dian smiled, very briefly. "Everything changed once I was, you know, discovered by Daniel Manheim," she said, folding her hands in her lap.

The producer, she explained to Groucho, had spotted her over a year ago and signed her to an exclusive long-term contract. Since then she hadn't appeared in a movie, concentrating instead on studying acting, dancing, and a wide range of other things that Manheim believed would improve her. His people had redesigned her, renamed her, and, when Manheim had decided she was ready, starred her in his very expensive production of *Saint Joan*.

Leaning back, Groucho steepled his fingers under his chin. "And what does your husband think about this miraculous transformation?"

She looked down at the folded hands. There wasn't any ring showing. "Jim and I are separated."

"Your idea?"

"I thought so at the time," she answered slowly. "But, it seems to me now that this was really Daniel Manheim's idea."

"And where's Jim?"

"Well, he's opening next week in a new play on Broadway," she said, allowing herself to smile for a few seconds. "It's a wonderful break for him. Jim's starring in that new mystery comedy, *Make Mine Murder*."

"I've heard of it. One of the few Broadway comedies that George S. Kaufman didn't write."

"I'm planning to see the play opening night," she said, defiance in her voice now.

"Manheim objects?"

She nodded. "Yes, he wants me to stay completely away from Jim," she said. "I know this will sound like melodramatic hokum, Groucho, but he really is a Svengali. Sometimes I think he wants to just control me completely."

"Has the guy made any passes at you?"

She shook her head. "Not really, no, but . . ."

"But what?"

"He's even more possessive than if he were my lover."

"What you ought to do, my dear, is—"

"Did you know Nick Sanantonio?"

Groucho elevated both eyebrows. "No, but my brother Chico did," he answered. "Chico, alas, is on cordial terms with all and sundry gamblers in southern California. He's contributed generously to their cause." He watched her for a moment. "Don't tell me that you were friends with a gangster like Sanantonio?"

"Not exactly, although I met him a few times while I was doing a picture at Warner's," the actress answered. "He was a good friend of George Raft."

"Many a hoodlum is. If you're going to specialize in saintly roles, kiddo, you ought not to hang around with the likes of the late Nick."

"I never actually hung around with him, Groucho," she assured him. "But I did know him casually and he was always very nice to me. When I read about his death in the paper this afternoon, I was really upset. That's a horrible way to die."

"True, but expiring in that style is one of the work-related hazards of Sanantonio's field of endeavor."

"I know, but still it's very brutal to be shot down in—"

The new knocking on his compartment door was far from timid. It came close to being a pounding.

"Do they have house detectives on the Super Chief?" Groucho slouched over to the door and tugged it open.

"Ah, I thought maybe I'd find my princess here." Manheim was

44

looking into the room, smiling in Dian's direction. "It's way past your bedtime, darling."

"I'll be back to my room in a few minutes, Daniel."

"I think now would be better, dear. You need to rest up for the ordeal that Manhattan will—"

"Let me paraphrase the immortal Voltaire, Manheim," said Groucho. "Scram or I'll punch you in the snoot."

The hefty white-haired producer gave Groucho a nasty smile. "That wouldn't be a very smart thing to try, Julius," he said. "Dian?"

"Soon," she said.

"Very well." He turned on his heel and started off down the swaying train corridor. "Don't be too long."

Leaving the chair, the young woman said to Groucho, "Joan of Arc is a marvelous part. It really will make me a star."

"Keep in mind how the real Joan of Arc ended up," he reminded.

Eight

Groucho couldn't sleep.

And he wasn't in the mood for any more T. S. Eliot.

So around 2:00 A.M., a little while after the speeding Super Chief had crossed into Arizona, he decided to stroll through the train and visit the baggage car.

Humming a few bars of "My True Love Lies Dead in the Baggage Coach Ahead," he shed his venerable robe and donned a tweedy sports coat. Groucho had packed an old orange crate with books and was shipping them to his New York hotel. Included in the shipment was a copy of S. J. Perelman's most recent book.

It was Groucho's intention to see if he could get into the baggage car and unpack a few books, including Perelman's, to bring back to his compartment.

"If reading Sid's book won't put me to sleep, nothing will," he said to himself as he opened the door.

The corridor was dim-lit, the only sound the rhythmic clacking of the train wheels on the tracks. Out the windows showed darkness and moonlit desert country.

Groucho discovered he wasn't the only one roaming the speeding Super Chief. Before he reached the door at the other end of the corridor, it came sliding open.

A thin, middle-aged woman entered and made a pleased noise when she recognized him. "Groucho Marx," she said, reaching into the large imitation-leather purse she was toting. "I'm a great fan of yours."

"Too bad you're not a fan dancer," he said. "A little hootchie-cootchie exhibition would liven up this long, dreary night."

She produced an autograph album from within her purse. "Can you write your name on a moving train?"

"Depends on how fast the train is moving," he replied. "This one, for example, is moving too fast for me to trot alongside and inscribe something on its panels. A slow milk train, however, I might be able to keep up with until—"

"I meant can you sign my book while the train's moving."

Somewhat gingerly, he accepted the proffered album and, producing a fountain pen from a pocket of his jacket, scrawled his name. He returned the book, saying, "And now, dear lady, I must continue my nocturnal mission. Farewell."

Two porters and a waiter were playing poker up in the cocktail lounge.

Further down in the car four members of the *Step Right Up* troupe, two men and two women, were gathered. The plumper guy was noodling quietly on a clarinet.

"Do anything for you, Mr. Marx?" asked one of the porters.

Groucho shook his head. "Pay no attention to me, lads. I'm merely walking in my sleep."

As he neared the group, the fellow with the clarinet started playing "Hurray for Captain Spaulding," Groucho's song from *Animal Crackers*.

Halting, Groucho bowed and then—or so he later told me—executed an extremely graceful pirouette before continuing on his way.

As he entered the next car, which was given over to the less expensive roomettes, a door opened. A pretty young girl dancer murmured, "Good night, Wally," and stepped out into the swaying corridor.

"Ah, romance," remarked Groucho with a sigh.

The dancer eased her roomette door open, then glanced over her shoulder at him. "And who are you visiting, Mr. Marx?"

"I understand they have an educated horse up in the baggage car," he answered.

At the quiet end of the car he encountered a dozing conductor. The man was lean, his cap resting in his narrow lap. He sat slumped on a seat in a roomette, his left foot keeping the sliding door half-open.

Groucho tiptoed by him.

The lights in the next car, which was given over to double bedrooms, were out.

It was while making his way gingerly along the dark swaying corridor that Groucho tripped over the body.

What the heck are you doing up there?" Jane inquired from below.

"Reading," I replied.

"That's supposed to be a relatively silent pastime."

"Having trouble settling into a comfortable position. Sorry."

Our compartment had a sort of upper berth–lower berth setup and, after parting for the evening, I'd climbed into the upper.

The monotonous clicking of the train on the rails didn't seem to soothe me and I kept waking up every few minutes. Finally, in the vicinity of 1:00 A.M., I clicked on my overhead bunk light, fished out the copy of *Dime Detective* I'd slipped under my pillow, and made an attempt to read a novelette about a very hard-boiled Hollywood private eye.

Jane had been comfortably asleep since about midnight, but my thrashing around woke her up.

"I suppose counting sheep wouldn't help?" she asked.

"Tried that," I said. "But before I could even get up to one hundred, a bunch of cattlemen rode over to warn me not to try counting sheep in cow country."

"Would you like to come down here again?"

"That isn't going to help me sleep."

"Nope, but it'll maybe help pass the time."

"True," I agreed, swinging out of my bunk.

As Groucho fell toward the floor of the train corridor, he thrust out both his hands, fingers wide. He hit with a hard jolt that sent pain snaking up his arms and across his chest.

"Oy," he exhaled, starting to untangle himself from the sprawled body.

Groucho struggled himself up to a sitting position, his eyes becoming used to the darkness.

The train whistle let out a long mournful hoot.

"I couldn't agree more," he muttered.

When he looked more closely at the body, he discovered that it was Hal Arneson and that he was only out cold and not dead.

Arneson was lying facedown on the corridor carpeting, breathing in a noisy nasal way.

Starting to rise, Groucho noticed a faint glow of light to his left.

The door to a bedroom had slid a few inches open and he saw a small flashlight floating in there a few feet above the floor. The light also caused what might be the blade of a knife to flash once.

Feeling momentarily foolhardy, Groucho eased closer to the open bedroom.

At the opening he called out, "Am I correct in assuming that you're up to no good in there?"

Suddenly the door snapped full open.

A dark figure with a scarf wrapped round its face came shoving into Groucho.

He saw a flicker of a knife in the right hand, then the flashlight in the left hand was shining right into his eyes.

The hand holding the light pushed him hard in the chest.

"Oof," he commented as he was shoved again, this time by a sharp elbow in his middle.

He gasped out breath, stumbled, fell back, and tripped once more over the snoring Arneson.

The dark figure ran swiftly down the corridor and was swallowed by the darkness. Seconds later the door at the corridor's end opened and shut.

"I should've stuck with *The Wasteland*," decided Groucho, rising yet again.

After hesitating in the bedroom doorway for a few seconds, he reached in to click on the lights. "Once more into the fray," he said and entered.

Daniel Manheim, clad in candy-stripe pajamas, was lying on his back in the bed.

The white-haired movie producer was unconscious, snoring profusely. There was no sign that the knife had been used on him.

The smell of something that was probably chloroform was strong all around him.

Groucho moved closer to the drugged man. "Time to rise and shine," he announced loudly.

Manheim went on slumbering.

Moving the rumpled Santa Fe blanket aside, Groucho scanned the hefty man. "Nope, nothing at all to indicate he's been stabbed anyplace important."

Groucho rubbed at his own chest, which was commencing to feel sore. Returning to the corridor, he crouched beside Arneson and tapped him on the arm. "How about you, King Kong?"

Just as the big man groaned, the beam of a powerful flashlight caught Groucho. "Here now, what's going on?" asked the lean conductor.

"We're giving a wide array of prizes to anyone who can answer that question in twenty-five words or less," Groucho said, standing to face him.

Nine

At about the same time that Groucho was having fun up near the front of the Super Chief, I was returning to a state of wakefulness. Upstairs again in my own bunk, I was fighting an impulse to turn on my light and shift my position again.

Finally, sighing very quietly, I lowered myself to the carpeted floor of our compartment. Slowly, in the dark and with as little noise as possible, I located my clothes and shoes where I'd neatly tossed them the night before.

I was nearly dressed when Jane asked, in a not-quite-awake voice, "Where you going?"

"Still can't sleep." Balancing on one foot, I tugged on a loafer. "Going to take a walk."

"Well, try to stay on the train."

"I may run alongside for a while, but that's as far afield as I intend to go."

"Be careful," she advised and returned to sleep.

I let myself out into the dimly illuminated corridor.

Walking toward the rear of the train, I made my way to the last car. Beyond the drawing rooms was the observation car.

This was done up in what a Santa Fe brochure called Navajo Indian style. It had a turquoise ceiling, the chairs were covered with material bearing what might have been Navajo designs, and there were Indian artworks on the sand-colored walls. The windows showed views of the flat moonlit Arizona countryside. The tall, many-armed cactuses made shadowy silhouettes out in the night.

The only other person in the car was Willa Jerome. The blonde actress was wearing slacks and a cardigan sweater over a striped blouse. Her legs were crossed, an open copy of the *New Yorker* steepled over one knee. Gazing out at the night we were rushing through, she was taking a deep drag on a cork-tipped cigarette.

"Morning," I said.

Turning, she exhaled smoke and bestowed a faint patrician smile on me. "Having trouble sleeping?"

"Yeah. I don't do well in strange bedrooms."

"I've slept in a great many strange bedrooms," she said, "but trains always give me the jitters. You're the newspaper man, aren't you?"

I sat down across from her. "Used to be. *Los Angeles Times,*" I answered. "But for the past three years—"

"Then you have absolutely no interest in interviewing me?"

"I don't have any yearnings in that direction, no."

"And you don't give a damn about what Tyrone Power is really like?"

"I know enough about Tyrone Power already to suffice me for a good many years to come."

Willa snuffed out her cigarette in a standing ashtray. "Your name is?"

"Frank Denby."

She nodded. "Seems to me I heard you did something unusual with the Marx Brothers."

"Actually, Groucho Marx and I have worked together. I wrote his radio show and we teamed up a few times to solve some real-life murder cases."

"Oh, yes, it's the murder part someone was telling me about," she said. "Does that pay well, that sort of detective work?"

"Doesn't pay anything at all," I replied. "We're what they call amateur detectives."

"And so you do it because . . . ?"

"I guess it's a mixture of altruism and showing off, Miss Jerome."

"Are you and Groucho traveling to New York to solve a new mystery, Frank?"

"Nope. It's purely a coincidence that we both happened to have business in Manhattan at the same time," I said. "He's going to be—"

"Your wife is quite pretty. That *is* your wife you're traveling with, isn't it?"

"Jane Danner's my wife, yes. I know it's the mark of a yokel to travel with your own wife and not somebody else's, but—"

"Oh, here's Emily. I hope she's not bringing me more telegrams from the blessed studio."

The plain young woman had come, very politely and carefully, into the swaying observation car. She, too, was wearing slacks. "Excuse me for interrupting, Willa," she apologized as she approached us. "But I thought you might like to see the additions to your Manhattan agenda that Zanuck's publicity people have been wiring us at various train stops."

"Emily Collinson, this is Frank Denby."

The secretary smiled politely at me. "It's a pity that you're not reporting for the *LA Times* any longer, Mr. Denby."

"I don't know if pity is exactly the word that applies."

Seating herself next to her boss, she handed Willa a typed sheet of paper. "We noticed you and your wife dining at El Perro Lindo this evening," she said across to me.

"Seems like several passengers dropped in there for a farewell meal. Such as Hal Arneson and—"

"A very outgoing man," observed the actress. She took a fresh cigarette from the box of them in her purse and Emily lit it for her. "We don't have very many people as exuberant as Hal in England, even in the cinema business. And his manner of dressing. Bright red necktie, ill-fitting suit. Not Savile Row by any means."

"He's amiable enough," Emily said.

"A flack has to be." Willa turned her attention to the amended agenda. "How in the bloody hell am I supposed to get from this radio interview at NBC on Tuesday morning over to WOR when they're practically simultaneous?"

Leaning, Emily tapped the sheet. "There's a fifteen-minute gap between them, Willa," she pointed out. "And Twentieth is providing a limousine to take us from spot to spot."

The actress was counting the list of interviews. "On that same day I'm scheduled to do eleven other interviews about *Trafalgar Square*," she said, shaking her head. "That's a good dozen too many."

"There's a great deal of interest in you, Willa, so—"

"Bullshit," she retorted. "This is just more manufactured flapdoodle that those morons in Hollywood try to inflict on me to—"

"Excuse my breaking in on your hen party, Frank," said Jane from the doorway. "But Groucho's sent word that he'd like to see you." She'd put on a terry-cloth robe over her nightgown.

"Something wrong?" Getting up, I started toward her.

She shook her head, shrugged. "I don't know for sure. He sent a porter with the message."

Turning toward Willa and her secretary, I said, "I've got to leave you, ladies."

"Another mystery, do you think?" asked the blonde actress.

"One never knows," I answered.

The lanky conductor had slowly lowered the beam of his flashlight from Groucho's face to the sprawled, and starting-to-stir, Arneson. "I didn't recognize you right off, Mr. Marx," he said apologetically. "Probably because you don't have your moustache."

"No, I usually put it in a glass of water at my bedside of an evening," he said, pointing at the groggy troubleshooter–publicity man. "Looks like somebody conked him on the coco with what is technically known as a blunt instrument."

The conductor crouched, checking Arneson's pulse. "Gave him a nasty bump on the back of his head." He straightened up. "They smashed the lightbulbs, too."

"You better take a look in Manheim's bedroom," suggested Groucho.

"My God, he isn't dead, is he?" The conductor hurried over to the large room.

"No, he's still extant, but somebody seems to have slipped him a mickey."

"He's out cold, sure enough," said the conductor.

"I'm no expert on how to stupefy movie moguls," said Groucho, who'd remained beside the fallen Arneson. "But I'd guess they used something like chloroform on him."

"Shit," murmured Arneson.

"Ah, a sign of life." Groucho leaned closer to him. "Want to try to rise, Harold?"

"Got slugged, huh?" said the husky man.

"That appears to be the case."

"Who did it?"

"Darn, we thought you were going to be able to provide us with that information." Groucho held out his hand.

Arneson took hold, pulling himself to a sitting position. He smoothed out his suit jacket, straightened out the red knit tie he'd apparently changed to since Groucho had last seen him. "No, hell no, Groucho," he said, his speech still slightly slurred, "I have no idea who it was. All I'm pretty certain of is that somebody came up behind me and bopped me good and hard."

"What were you doing out here in the corridor?"

"My bedroom's next to Manheim's and . . . Jesus, is he okay?" He struggled to his feet.

"He's all right, though unconscious. Granted many motion picture

57

producers are perennially in that condition, but in Manheim's case it was probably chloroform that did it."

Wobbly, Arneson took a few steps toward the bedroom doorway. The train gave a sudden lurch and he thrust out his hand to steady himself against the wall. "I prowl quite a bit nighttimes," he explained. "To see that everything's okay. This time . . . well, I got knocked out before I realized anything was going on wrong."

"Out like a light," announced the conductor from within the bedroom. "I'm not sure why he was knocked out, Mr. Arneson. You better come in, see if anything was stolen."

"I saw somebody bending over him with a knife," mentioned Groucho, taking a cigar out of his coat pocket.

"Then possibly you interrupted a murder attempt," said the conductor. "I'll notify the authorities to meet us when we stop at Flagstaff. They'll investigate this whole mess and—"

"Wait now." Arneson pushed into the bedroom, glanced at his unconscious boss, and nodded. He put a hand on the conductor's arm. "What's your name again?"

"Hopkins. Leonard Hopkins."

"Okay, Leonard. Here's the situation," said the big man. "We don't want this sort of publicity just now."

"But there's been an attack on you and Mr. Manheim, possibly a murder attempt," protested Hopkins. "I simply can't let it—"

"Sure, you can, Leonard," cut in Arneson. "It's not going to please Mr. Manheim, when he comes to his senses again, to find out that you've made a big stink about what is, far as I can see, a minor incident. We're about to introduce a major new actress to the world. Unsubstantiated crap about a juvenile prank played aboard your train isn't going to do us any good."

"Even so, Mr. Arneson—"

"And, as you probably know, Mr. Manheim is a very good friend of several of your Santa Fe railroad executives," continued Arneson, moving his hand from the conductor's arm to his shoulder. "I'm not saying

58

that annoying Mr. Manheim is going to affect your position with the Super Chief, Leonard, but it's not likely it'll do you a hell of a lot of good."

After a few silent seconds, Hopkins said, quietly, "I suppose, if you and Mr. Manheim don't intend to make a complaint about what's happened, well, then I can probably forget this."

Arneson grinned and let go of the conductor. "Mr. Manheim's going to be pleased by your decision, Leonard."

The conductor looked down at the snoring producer, frowning. "But we'd best have a doctor look at him."

"That won't be necessary," Arneson assured him. "I have some experience along that line. You just see about replacing those damaged lightbulbs, Leonard, and then forget all about this." He lurched over to the doorway to eye Groucho. "Be nice if you didn't blab about this either."

"Mum's the word," promised Groucho, bowing slightly in his direction. "Not much of a word, but one of the few I can think of at this ungodly hour. Good evening, one and all."

Ten

Groucho, as best he could, paced his relatively small compartment while he recounted to Jane and me what had befallen him when he attempted to visit the baggage car. He paced in a sort of shuffling slouch, unlit cigar between his teeth, hands clasped behind his back.

I was leaning against the wall, Jane was sharing the couch with Groucho's guitar case.

"And that, kiddies, concludes tonight's episode of *I Love a Mystery Not to Mention Three Awfully Cute Sailors,*" he announced when he reached the end of his account.

Jane watched him for a few seconds, then asked, "Are you all right?"

"Well, I must admit I seem to be suffering from an acute case of the wimwams, but other than that—"

"I mean this would-be assassin knocked you down," she amplified. "Did you get hurt?"

"I've taken so many tumbles that I'm immune to injury, my dear, but thanks for asking," he said.

"Do you have any idea who it was?"

"Not much, Professor Quiz. Middle-sized, not tall. Since there was a minimum of illumination at the time, I didn't see any details."

Jane said, "Man or woman?"

Groucho narrowed his left eye and gazed at the ceiling of the compartment. "A man, I'm pretty certain. Although I wouldn't swear to it in court. Although the last time I swore in court they washed out my mouth with soap and gave me thirty days. And you should've seen the days they gave me. Why, at least a dozen of them were Mondays and extremely moth-eaten. But, then, so was I."

I asked, "Are you thinking about our looking into this incident?"

"No, definitely not, nope, nosiree." Groucho held up his right hand in a halt-right-there gesture. "I might also add nay and not at all. This will be a detection-free sojourn. I merely, since you've occasionally served as my Boswell—that's James not Connee—was anxious to fill you in on what's been occurring in my rich and eventful life. The next event, by the way, will be the Annual Strawberry Festival, which will commence just the minute the strawberry in question arrives from far-off—"

"When I referred to this guy as an assassin, you didn't correct me," put in Jane. "Do you fellas believe that somebody tried to murder Manheim?"

Halting and frowning in my wife's direction, Groucho said, "It makes no nevermind, Little Dorrit. The firm of Marx and Denby—Ratiocination While You Wait—isn't interested in whether or not somebody attempted to bump off a *mamzer* like Manheim. I only wanted to inform you of—"

"Seems to me," she said, "that you can't pick and choose, Groucho. I think you two ought to look into this some more, because maybe next time this mystery man will succeed in killing him. I wouldn't want something like that on my conscience."

Groucho lit his cigar, slowly. Then he nodded in my direction. "What's your opinion, Rollo?" he asked. "Are we obliged to protect Manheim?"

I took a slow breath in and out. "We can at least poke around a little," I told him. "Even though, from what you told us, Arneson wants to keep the lid on this."

Jane said, "That's something else you two might think about. Why's a publicity man so eager to cover this up?"

I said, "That's what a troubleshooter is supposed to do, Jane. Keep scandals hidden, see that the newspapers don't find out about embarrassing—"

"But that's just it," she persisted. "Why is this embarrassing? You could get a lot of swell publicity from it. You know, 'Producer of *Saint Joan* Victim of Mystery Attack,' 'En Route to Introducing Dian Bowers to World, Manheim Attacked by Mystery Assailant.' "

"That last one's way too long for a headline."

"So make it a subhead. You ought to be wondering why Arneson doesn't want this to get out."

Groucho exhaled smoke. "What's your theory, Nancy Drew?"

"Well, it could be that the guy knows more than he's letting on."

"Knows who it was who assaulted him and Manheim?" I said.

"Maybe so. But, listen, you fellas are the detectives, remember?" she said, grinning. "I'm only a gadfly. And a sleepy one at that."

Groucho had commenced pacing again, a bit more slowly than before. "One thing to establish is what was actually afoot in Manheim's bedroom," he said. "Somebody rendered him unconscious with chloroform. And that somebody was seen, by a reliable witness—one Julius Marx, unemployed steeplejack—in the producer's vicinity clutching what looked very much like a knife."

I said, "That somebody also knocked Arneson out, probably with a blackjack. Then he goes in and chloroforms Manheim, so that he can then take his time stabbing him and making sure he hits a vital spot."

"What about the lights in the corridor?" asked Jane.

"Hm?" I inquired.

"Why did the mystery man put out the lights in the corridor."

"So he could sneak up on Arneson, probably," I answered.

"The lights were on when Arneson got slugged," said Groucho. "Besides, it would be difficult to smash the lights without attracting the guy's attention, since he was patrolling the area."

"So he bops him, goes in and drugs Manheim, comes back out to put the lights on the fritz, then goes back in to try his stabbing?"

"He no doubt wanted to work under the cover of as much darkness as possible—one reason he brought a flashlight along," said Groucho, dropping into a chair.

Jane snapped her fingers. "Hey, suppose there were two people involved," she said, straightening up. "One to deck our erstwhile football player, the other to go in and knife Manheim."

Groucho shook his head. "I didn't see anybody else lurking around."

"It was dark," reminded Jane.

"Arneson's a former fullback," I said. "If a former fullback falls over in the corridor, wouldn't somebody have heard it?"

"Is this one of those philosophical speculations," asked Groucho, "like the one about the tree falling in the forest?"

"Apparently Manheim didn't hear anything," said Jane. "It might be worthwhile to talk to the other passengers in that car. Does this protégée of his, Dian Bowers, have a bedroom in that same car, for instance?"

"Am I correct in concluding that you think we should go ahead and investigate this sordid incident?" Groucho asked me.

"It'll help us pass the time on the trip," I pointed out.

"Okay, but I prefer cribbage," said Groucho. "Or, if worse comes to worst, corned beef and cribbage."

"What about motive?" said Jane.

"Our motive, according to your common-law hubby, is to avoid playing cribbage and enjoying scenic America while rushing eastward in this streamlined cattle car."

"I mean the motive for killing Manheim. Any notions?"

"A recent survey conducted by the Mind Your Own Beeswax Foundation of Petaluma determined that well over fifty percent of the people in the movie business have good reason to loathe Manheim and wish him dead," said Groucho, puffing on his cigar. "We're going to have to work some to narrow that list down. I'd also estimate that half the people on this streamliner don't like him."

"The dancer," said Jane.

"You think maybe?" I said to my wife.

"He'd be on my list if I were a sleuth, yes."

"Oh, what fun," said Groucho, clapping his hands together. "I just love guessing what in the blue blazes you two pixies are babbling about."

I explained about the young dancer who'd heckled the movie producer during the platform press conference. "His first name is Len," I wound up.

"I've been able to establish diplomatic relations with several of the young ladies in the *Step Right Up* dance troupe," said Groucho. "I'll make a few discreet inquiries come morning."

Jane yawned a small yawn. "Morning's not that far off," she said, standing. "We better think about turning in, Frank."

"Go right ahead, you young folks," said Groucho. "I'll be just simply fine all alone here in my cell, with only my memories and those tusks we brought back from our last expedition to Tarzana."

Jane crossed to him, kissed him on the forehead, and said, "Send for us if you fall over again, Groucho."

I said good night and we went along the corridor to our compartment.

Eleven

The next morning, as the speeding streamliner was approaching Gallup, New Mexico, Groucho came slouching into the slightly swaying dining car and seated himself next to the pretty red-haired dancer. Her name was Franki Rafferty and Groucho had, he later told me, arranged to meet her for breakfast so he could gather information. "And I wasn't above gathering a few rosebuds while I might," he added.

Outside the diner windows showed an immense stretch of desert, dotted with prickly organ-pipe cactus and spiky yucca plants.

"No funny stuff," Franki warned as Groucho dropped into the chair next to hers.

Groucho straightened up, assuming a fairly convincing maligned expression. "Funny stuff? I'd like to see the man who dares accuse Groucho Marx of being funny."

"I mean funny stuff of a hugging, pinching kind, Groucho," Franki amplified. "Everything'll be hunky-dory if you keep both hands in plain sight at all times. Okay?"

He sighed. "It's going to make it more difficult for me to guess your weight, my child," he said. "But so be it."

She returned to studying the menu. "I take it you're picking up the tab?"

"I'll have you know that the Marx clan is famed throughout the

South for never allowing a lady to pick up a check," he assured her. "Of course, I think it only fair to warn you that we're not in the South at the moment."

"I think I'll have the French toast."

Consulting his menu, Groucho said, "I suppose we can afford that," he decided. "I don't see any gruel listed on the bill of fare, so I'll have—"

"Pardon me, Mr. Marx." A plump middle-aged woman in a flowered dress had stopped beside their table, a small box camera held tightly in both hands.

"Ah, I see they've taken to heart the note I dropped in the suggestion box on my last trip and have added gorgeous waitresses to their staff. We'll have—"

"No, I'm a fellow passenger," she corrected. "May I take your picture?"

Groucho leaned back in his chair, took a cigar from his breast pocket. "That's going to depend, dear lady, on which picture you want to take," he informed her as he unwrapped the cigar. "The framed Varga girl I have in a place of honor over my bedstead I'd miss a lot. However, the dying cowboy that hangs over the mantel in the living room you can swipe whenever you're in the neighborhood. His horse is wall-eyed and—"

"No, I meant," she said, holding up the camera, "I want to take your picture with my Brownie."

He shook his head. "Alas, due to an onerous clause in my contract, I'm not allowed to be photographed with elves, gnomes, trolls, or brownies," he explained. "However, should you care to snap an informal portrait of me and this far-from-zaftig young lady, why, shoot if you must."

"That's what I had in mind, Mr. Marx," she said, looking down at him through the camera.

"Hands in plain sight," reminded Franki as Groucho started to put an avuncular arm around her.

The plump woman snapped two quick pictures, thanked him, and went back to her place a few tables away.

After the waiter took their written breakfast orders, Groucho got to the real point of this get-together. "Forgive an old man's curiosity, Francesca, but I'm eager for information about some of the other members of your gifted ensemble."

"So you did have an ulterior motive for inviting me to breakfast, huh?"

"Yes, I did," he confessed. "But that's better than a posterior motive, which is what often drives my—"

"Maggie was right."

"Is she one of the blondes?"

"At the moment, yeah. She told me that you're probably playing detective again," said Franki. "Because of that attack on Manheim."

His eyebrows rose. "You lasses know about that?"

"C'mon, Groucho, it's all over the darn train."

Dropping the unlit cigar back into his pocket, he asked her, "Any ideas about who'd try to do him harm?"

"Ask me, it's a publicity stunt. To promote that flat-chested latest discovery of his. Joan of Arc, my fanny."

Groucho observed, "A somewhat drastic way to get publicity."

"Manheim, so I hear, is a pretty drastic guy."

Groucho asked, "What about the chap who heckled him in Union Station yesterday?"

"Len Cowan?" She gave a shake of her head. "He's just a harmless hothead. I've worked with Len before—a year or so ago at RKO—and he's the kind of guy who's always flying off the handle. But he limits himself to yelling and making scenes and doesn't go in for physical assaults."

"Who was the Kathy Sutter he alluded to?"

Franki looked out the window, watching the bright morning desert rush by. "Well, her real name was Kathy Cowan."

"Len's wife?"

"Sister."

"What happened to her?" asked Groucho, resting an elbow on the tabletop. "And how does it tie in with Manheim?"

"It was about two years ago," she said. "Kathy was . . . hell, she was no more than twenty-two or twenty-three." She took a slow breath in and out. "Manheim discovered her, too."

"But something went wrong?"

"Yeah, just about everything," Franki answered. "Kathy had never gotten out of the chorus, but she'd studied ballet since she was a kid. Anyway, Manheim noticed her. See, he was planning to do an epic about Pavlova and he had a hunch he could turn Kathy into a star and that she'd be perfect for the leading role. She became one more of his discoveries and he groomed her, had his people remodel her and . . . well, they became lovers for a while."

Groucho nodded.

Franki said, "After about five months Manheim decided he wasn't going to make a Pavlova flicker after all. From that moment he wasn't interested anymore in having her at his studio or in his bed."

Frowning deeply, Groucho said, "I remember her now, reading about her in the papers. She—"

"Killed herself, yeah. Swam out into the Pacific from Santa Monica one night until she couldn't swim anymore," said Franki quietly. "Then she drowned. A nice Hollywood finish."

"And her brother blames Manheim for her death."

"Sure, wouldn't you?" she said. "Kathy, poor kid, was sort of soft and not very sure of herself. Me, I would have spit in Manheim's eye and told him where he could stuff Pavlova. But Kathy . . . she just gave up."

"Did you folks know that Manheim was going to be traveling on this particular Super Chief?"

"Sure, it was in all the trades. Don't you read them?"

"I can only afford to subscribe to *Nick Carter's Weekly,* I fear."

When the breakfasts arrived, Franki looked down at her plate and then shook her head. "Funny, I don't feel hungry at all, Groucho. Think I'll head back to my roomette." She pushed back from the table.

"If you don't mind, my child, I won't escort you," he said, watching her get up. "Someone had better stay here and look after all this French toast."

While Groucho was occupied in the diner, I headed up through the train toward the bedroom car where Manheim had his trouble. Groucho had suggested that I talk to Dian Bowers and find out what she knew about the attack.

Making my way through the car that housed the roomettes—which even Santa Fe literature described as tiny—I had to dodge wandering members of the *Step Right Up* bunch, who were room-hopping, heading for the dining car, or simply loitering.

A blonde, freckled dancer signaled me as I passed her open roomette. "You're a friend of Groucho Marx, aren't you?"

I halted. "Yeah," I admitted.

She was wearing a white imitation satin robe and not much lingerie under it. "Are you in the movie business?"

"Not at the moment, no."

After making a disappointed noise, she inquired, "What then?"

"Radio," I answered.

"Not much work for hoofers in radio."

"Nope," I agreed. "We have soundmen to provide the tap dancing."

"Then there's not much point in my vamping you."

"Just about none at all."

"See you around, kid." She slid her door shut and I continued on my way.

I was passing the rest room at the car's end when the tan curtain that masked the door parted. A large hand came shooting out and caught my sleeve.

"Hold it a minute, junior."

Hal Arneson was attached to the fist that was detaining me.

"I already shaved and washed up, Hal, so you don't have to drag me into the—"

"You wouldn't, would you, Denby, be on your way to try to annoy Mr. Manheim or Miss Bowers, huh?"

I shrugged free of his grasp. "Groucho was anxious to know how you two fellows were feeling after your ordeal of last night," I lied. "He was also concerned about how Dian Bowers was faring and—"

"As you can see for yourself, buddy, I'm in great shape," Arneson told me, stepping fully out into the corridor. "Mr. Manheim, Groucho will be pleased to learn, is resting comfortably in his private bedroom. Notice the word *private*."

"He came out of his stupor?"

"He's just fine. Don't worry about it, Denby. You or Groucho."

"And how about Dian Bowers?"

"How about her?"

"Groucho was wondering if all that action in the corridor last night disturbed her," I said. "Seeing as how her bedroom is just two down from Manheim's, Groucho wanted to make sure she got back to sleep after—"

"It's not you know, really any of his god damn business," cut in the big man. "I will tell you, though, so Groucho doesn't fret, that Miss Bowers didn't see or hear a damned thing. She doesn't sleep very well on trains—he can understand that, I imagine—and Mr. Manheim had his physician prescribe a sedative for her to use on the trip. Dian Bowers slept through the whole business, Denby."

"Didn't see or hear anything?"

"Exactly. Now why don't you go back and have breakfast with that charming wife of yours?"

"Splendid idea," I said and withdrew.

Twelve

In Spanish the word *ratón* means mouse. At about half past three that afternoon, as the train was pulling out of Raton, New Mexico, there was a polite tapping on the door of our compartment.

Jane had been saying, "What mouse do you suppose it was named after?"

"Probably not Mickey." I moved to the door and slid it open a few inches.

Johnson the porter was standing politely out there. "Message for you, Mr. Denby," he said, handing me an envelope that looked to have several sheets of paper folded up within.

Accepting the envelope, I handed him a quarter. "Thanks."

"From Groucho?" asked my wife.

I shut the door. "Nope. The envelope says it's from Daniel Manheim Productions of Burbank, California."

"Want to bet it isn't an offer to go to work for him as a writer?"

I sat down in our chair and slit the envelope open with my thumb. "Arneson probably informed him that I was trying to talk to Dian Bowers," I said, "and this is to shoo me off."

There were four folded sheets of Daniel Manheim Productions stationery. What I had was a carbon copy of a typed memo he'd apparently sent to Groucho.

"Well?" asked Jane.

"It's addressed to Groucho with a copy to me," I answered after scanning the first page. "Or rather—To: Mr. Marx, cc: Mr. Denby."

She made a keep-going gesture with her right hand. "Some details?"

"Well, Manheim starts off with 'Let me express my sincerest appreciation to you, Groucho, for coming to my assistance during the unfortunate incident that apparently took place on this very train late last evening. I appreciate as well—which goes without saying—your timely intercession on behalf of my associate, Mr. Arneson.' And then there's another long paragraph wherein he says that all over again in slightly different terms."

"This is what then—a very windy thank-you note?"

I was glancing at the other pages. "Not exactly, Jane."

"Okay, what's the gist of it?"

"You'll have to wait until tomorrow when we broadcast that on *Gist Plain Bill*."

"Oh, boy," she said, groaning delicately. "You're coming down with another bad case of Grouchoitis."

"Sorry," I apologized. "Would you prefer *Beau Gist*?"

"I'd prefer to know why in the heck Manheim is sending out bulky memos to you and Groucho."

"Okay, he goes on to say that he 'sincerely believes that the incident that took place in my bedroom last evening was more than likely the work of some deranged crank who climbed aboard the Super Chief during one of its many nighttime stops and then jumped off again after being thwarted.' "

"Think Manheim actually believes that?"

"It's what he wants us to believe," I said, tapping the memo pages. "The point of this all being that 'it's come to my attention that you and your associate, Mr. Denby, have been making admittedly discreet inquiries into the matter. This is being done, I hasten to point out, without my permission or approval. I must, therefore, respectfully request that you both cease any such activities and allow, as Mr. Arneson tells me he informed you last evening, this unpleasant occurrence to be forgotten. Should I decide at a later date that any action should be taken, I will do so without any assistance from either you or Mr. Denby.' "

"Somewhere in all that verbiage there's a polite brush-off," said Jane.

I nodded, resting the pages on my knee. "Yeah, and he also warns us, politely and with considerable circumlocution, to stay away from Dian Bowers for the rest of the trip."

Jane stood up, smoothed her tweed skirt and sat down again on the narrow sofa. "They don't, for whatever reason, want you fellows nosing around."

I folded the memo and put it back in the envelope. "Earlier we were talking about it sort of being our duty to dig into this business," I said. "You implied that Groucho and I were pretty much in the same category as the Lone Ranger and Tonto. But it's damn clear now that Manheim and Arneson really don't want our help."

"That's how I'd interpret the memo, yes."

"Okay, then. From now until New York, I'll concentrate on dreaming up socko scenarios for our forthcoming *Hollywood Molly* radio show and not dabble in detection."

"Might as well," agreed Jane. "Manheim doesn't realize what he's missing, though. You and Groucho are pretty good detectives." She stood again, stretching. "And I'm still kind of curious to find out what really happened and why."

"So am I," I admitted. "But I'm damned if I'll try to force Manheim and Arneson to let us go on investigating this."

"Think Groucho will agree to abandoning the whole thing?"

"I'll go find out," I said, getting up, sticking the envelope in my coat pocket, and heading for the door.

Groucho was seated in the cocktail lounge demurely reading a copy of *The Woman's Home Companion,* his guitar case leaning inconspicuously against the wall near his chair.

He became aware, after a moment, that someone was standing in front of him.

Lowering his magazine, he saw a plump grey-haired woman gazing, with furrowed brow, down at him. "Just the sort of person I want to see," said Groucho. "I'm dreadfully anxious to try this new recipe for pineapple upside-down cake. But, alas, the last time I attempted an upside-down cake, I got it backwards and ended with a right-side-up cake. It was terribly embarrassing, because my smart-set friends were expecting an upside-down cake and when I offered them a mundane right-side-up cake, they were deeply offended. And, much to my chagrin, I also discovered that I was two friends short of a complete set. What I need, therefore, is your expert advice on—"

"Could you help me settle a bet?" the woman interrupted shyly.

"Gambling is a dreadful habit, dear lady," he warned. "My brother Chico, for example, is shunned by polite society because of his unfortunate—"

"It's a bet I made with my husband," she continued. "He says it isn't you, but aren't you Groucho Marx without your moustache?"

"Ah, no, without my moustache I'm Tom Mix," he replied. "With my moustache I am sometimes Groucho Marx and other times Harriet Beecher Stowe or Grover Whalen, depending on the weather. And without a song the day would never end."

"Then you *are* Groucho Marx?"

He lowered his voice. "Just between us, my dear, I am indeed," he confided. "But I'll deny it in court."

She smiled, somewhat perplexed, and returned to her husband and her highball.

Groucho returned to his magazine.

It was suddenly yanked out of his hands by an angry young man. "I'm Len Cowan," he announced, scowling.

"Maybe *you* can help me with my upside-down-cake problem," said Groucho. "Or did you skulk over to beg me to sing "Lydia the Tattooed Lady" yet again? I understand the tune will soon be climbing up the

Hit Parade list, which is somewhat better than climbing up a slippery elm or—"

"Quit poking your nose in my business," warned the young dancer.

"Is this a threat? I hope so, because I always say there's nothing that livens up a dull journey like a threat from an impetuous young nitwit."

"I'm not interested in jokes, Groucho. What I—"

"Then you ought to flock to *At the Circus* when it's released," he advised. "Not a joke in a carload."

Cowan gave him a lopsided glare, his hands fisting. "You've been asking people questions about me."

"You've got me mixed up with Professor Quiz."

"If you've got something to ask, ask me to my face, damn it."

"I will, my lad, soon as you and your whiskey breath get downwind."

"Ask me, damn you."

"Okay. Did you attack Hal Arneson and Daniel Manheim last night?"

"None of your damned business."

"With answers like that, you ought to be able to understand why I have to go to strangers for my—"

"How'd you like a poke in the nose?"

"Is this an essay question or multiple choice?"

"Don't try these wiseass answers on—"

"Go and sit down," I suggested. I'd come into the cocktail lounge about twenty seconds earlier, hunting for Groucho.

"Who the hell are you?" demanded Cowan, turning to glare at me.

Quietly I said, "I'm the guy who's going to escort you the hell out of here in a very rough way, Cowan, unless you scram right now."

"Another damn fascist," he muttered. Staggering slightly, he made his way out of the car.

"Maybe you ought not to carry that guitar around with you," I suggested to Groucho as I settled into the chair next to his. "It seems to inspire attacks and assaults."

"True, but the open case comes in handy for catching money when

77

people throw pennies," he said, locating a cigar in one of the pockets of his mustard-colored sports jacket. "Am I correct in assuming that you also have perused a copy of Manheim's latest memo, which literary critics have certified as being nearly a thousand words longer than *Remembrance of Things Past*?"

"I read the whole thing, yeah."

"May we have your conclusions, Rollo?"

"I've got nothing against going around doing good deeds," I answered. "But I've decided we might as well quit working on this whole Manheim mess."

"My sentiments exactly," Groucho said. "I intend to devote my time henceforward to astronomy, quilting, and Honeymoon Bridge."

"Fine," I said.

He lit his cigar and blew a wispy smoke ring. "But I don't think Manheim's troubles are over," he said.

Thirteen

My troubles weren't over either. I didn't come to grief, though, until late that night, somewhere in the vicinity of Hutchinson, Kansas.

When Jane and I came back from having dinner with Groucho, I was saying, "He's fairly generous after all."

"Offering to treat everybody in the dining car to water isn't my idea of generosity."

I eased our door open. "I was referring to the fact that he paid for our dinners."

"After lecturing us on the many virtues of fasting."

I clicked on the lights. "Hello! What's this?"

Jane eyed me. "Nobody says that in real life."

"All too true," I admitted, genuflecting and picking up the pale blue envelope I'd noticed lying on the floor of our compartment. "But I've always admired the way British sleuths exclaim that in B movies."

She wrinkled her nose. "Jasmine."

"Yep, it sure smells right pretty, and it's addressed to me."

"Would you like me to step out into the corridor while you read it?"

"It's our policy to share all our clandestine affairs." Opening the envelope, I extracted the sheet of pale blue notepaper enclosed. "It's from Willa Jerome."

The actress's name was printed in a delicate typeface in the left-hand corner of the page.

"Is she maybe looking for a screenwriter?"

"She says, and I quote, 'If you meet me in the observation car tonight at eleven, I can tell you something important about what's been going on. Your Friend, Willa J.' " I let the hand holding the letter drop to my side. "Gosh, an audience with the star of *Trafalgar Square.*"

"It was my impression at dinner that you and Groucho were dropping this case." Jane sat on the sofa.

"We are, we did," I said. "But even so, Jane, if she knows something about who tried to knife Manheim, maybe I ought to go talk to her."

"I think slim, pretty witnesses are always more fun to interview than dumpy—"

"Hey, you come tag along with me," I invited. "If this were some kind of romantic interlude, she wouldn't want to meet me in the observation car. Where people could observe us."

"I trust you, Frank," Jane assured me. "You can go to your rendezvous solo."

"Okay, I guess I will." I went over to the window, spread a couple of the Venetian blind slats apart, and gazed out at the growing darkness we were traveling into.

A few minutes after eleven Groucho, he later told me, was settled in his compartment. Well, not exactly settled, since he was pretty sure he was going to have another night of insomnia.

"A sleeping potion might prove useful," he said to himself. "Although a love potion would also help while away the wee hours of the night."

He opened the small narrow clothes closet to select a sports coat. Because of the motion of the speeding streamliner, the coats were swinging gently on their hangers. He caught a nubby earth-brown jacket and put it on.

"Perhaps I can kill an hour or two in the observation car," he decided, unlocking his door and stepping out into the corridor.

The clacking of the wheels on the tracks sounded louder out here.

As he pushed open the door leading to the passageway connecting our car with the observation car, Groucho became aware of a faint groaning.

He squatted, staring into the shadows.

There was an unconscious man huddled there.

It was me.

"Frank!" recognized Groucho.

I groaned again.

As Groucho leaned closer, he saw the sheet of white paper that had been left on my chest.

It read, "Quit now!"

I became completely conscious to find a plump, white-haired man feeling the back of my head.

"I don't believe," I managed to say in a voice that I didn't quite recognize, "in phrenology."

"Returning to ourself, are we?" he asked in a sympathetic voice.

"Who exactly are you?" My voice was sounding more like my own.

"I'm Dr. Mackinson," he told me.

"He's the best we could find on such short notice," explained Groucho, who I now noticed was crouching next to the concerned doctor.

I also noticed that I was still on the floor of the passageway. "Where's Jane?"

"Right here, darling." She was standing just behind Groucho. "Groucho came and got me soon as he found you, then we asked the conductor to find a doctor. You okay?"

"I think I might be."

"How many fingers am I holding up?" inquired the doctor.

"Three," I replied. "Does anybody have any idea what actually happened to me?"

"I'm hoping you'll be able to provide some details on that." A uniformed conductor stepped out of the shadows beside my wife.

"Don't you have any idea, Frank?" asked Jane.

"All I'm certain about is that I got hit on the head." I winced as Dr. Mackinson shined his pocket flashlight into my eyes, left first, then right. "When I entered this damn passage, I heard a sort of rustling behind me and then . . . and then I was slugged, hard, from behind. That's it, until now."

"Possibly you," suggested the conductor, "were robbed."

"Of what? I left my wallet and money in our compartment with my wife."

"My colleague obviously has no notion of what befell him," put in Groucho, straightening up. "If it's okay by the sawbones here, I suggest we help Frank back to his quarters. You can interrogate him in the morning when he's feeling peppier and—"

"I understand *you* were involved in a similar incident last evening, Mr. Marx," said the conductor.

"In both instances I was nothing more than an innocent bystander," Groucho assured him. "Now, Doc, can we haul him off?"

"Yes, that will be all right." The doctor studied Groucho for a few seconds. "I didn't realize I was addressing one of the famous Marx Brothers. Which one are you?"

"Quacko, the medical member of the family. Frank's okay then?"

"Yes. He's not likely to suffer more than a bad headache."

"I really ought to fill out a report," complained the conductor.

"Tomorrow will do." Groucho and Jane helped me to rise to an upright position again.

I felt pretty wobbly. Putting an arm around Jane, I recalled where I had been heading when I got conked. "What about my meeting with Willa?"

"She's not in the observation car," said Jane. "I checked. Never was."

I glanced toward Groucho. "Looks like we're still involved with something."

"Apparently so," he agreed. "I just wish to hell I knew what it was."

Fourteen

The rattling of the train wheels on the tracks had started keeping time with the moderately painful throbbing of my injured head. I groaned quietly, opened my eyes somewhat, and looked down from my upper berth.

"Good morning," said Jane, who was sitting on the edge of her lower berth. "Welcome to Galesburg, Ohio."

"How's that again, girlie?"

"Something I read out the window awhile ago," she explained. "Seemed like a touching sentiment."

"That it is." I sat up as best I could and saw small zigzags of colored light for several unsettling seconds.

"Are you all right?" She stood up clear of her bed, looked up at me with concern.

"You know, ever since I went into the amateur detective line with Groucho," I observed, wincing, "I seem to be getting hit on the head quite a lot."

"Perhaps there's a moral there someplace. You feeling worse?"

"Nope, I believe I'm on the mend," I assured her. "By the way, why are my sports coats draped over the chair?"

"I was searching for that note you got last night."

"The one supposedly from Willa Jerome?"

"That note, uh huh. Couldn't find the darn thing, though."

"As I recall, I stuck it in the pocket of my plaid coat there before heading for my rendezvous with a blackjack." Very carefully, like someone who suddenly finds himself up on a skyscraper girder, I got myself down out of the upper bunk and onto the swaying compartment floor. "It's not there?"

"No. Whoever slugged you must've frisked you and retrieved it."

Feeling a mite woozy, I thrust out my hand against the wall to steady myself. "You said that Willa really didn't summon me?"

"So she told me last night."

"Meaning I was lured by persons unknown."

She nodded, reaching down to her bed for a slip of paper. "This is the warning that Groucho found stuck to you," she said, holding it toward me. "I was hoping to compare it with the handwriting on the note."

Jane's very good at identifying handwriting and lettering styles. Has to do with her being a cartoonist and exceptionally bright as well. Or at least that's my opinion. You may recall that she helped us that way when Groucho and I were working on that Sherlock Holmes mess last year.

"Any notion about who wrote this warning note?"

She gave an unhappy shake of her head. "Simple block letters and whoever did it was a right-hander using the left hand," she said. "Outside of that, nothing."

"Man or woman?"

"Can't be sure."

" 'Quit now!' That's awfully good advice. Some people would have to pay big money for such a helpful suggestion."

Dropping the note back onto the bed, Jane said, "I think maybe you really ought to quit, Frank. The next time they—"

"Hey, I am officially resigned from the whole Manheim business," I assured her.

"You certain?"

"Pretty much so, yeah."

Out in the train corridor the guy with the chimes went by. "First call to breakfast. First call to breakfast."

"Oops," said Jane, snapping her fingers. "We agreed to meet Groucho for breakfast."

"I was figuring that I'd feel more chipper this morning than I actually do."

"I'll go to the dining car, tell him you're not up to—"

"No, that's okay. I can make it," I told her. "You go ahead and I'll join you in about ten minutes. I just have to dress, shave, and put a plaster cast on my skull."

Giving me a slightly maternal smile, she kissed me on the cheek and left the room.

I was close to finishing up with my electric razor when there was a tapping on the door. Unplugging the razor, I moved to the doorway. I slid the door open very carefully.

"I hope I'm not disturbing you, Mr. Denby." It was Emily Collinson, Willa Jerome's secretary.

"Nope. C'mon in."

"I'll remain in the corridor," she said, pushing her glasses up on her nose. "Miss Jerome heard that you were injured last night while responding to a note that purported to be from her."

"That's what happened, yes."

Concern touched her pale face. "She didn't, of course, send you a message of any sort," the secretary said. "We did discover, though, that someone broke into our compartment during dinner last evening. The only thing stolen was a packet of Miss Jerome's personal stationery."

"No idea of by whom?"

She shook her head, unhappy that she couldn't provide me with any information about that. "None at all, sorry."

"Well, I appreciate your—"

"Miss Jerome instructed me to inquire as to whether you'd like to have her personal physician, Dr. Dowling, take a look at your head."

"I already had a Dr. Mackinson do that last night, thanks. He says it's nothing too serious."

"Just as well," said Emily. "Judging by his behavior last evening, Dr. Dowling is likely to be severely hungover most of today. I know I wouldn't want him poking around with my head."

I grinned. "We won't mention that to Miss Jerome."

She moved a step away. "You don't work for newspapers anymore?"

"I'm concentrating on radio and movies."

"You have a good prose style. Your *Los Angeles Times* columns were excellent."

"They weren't bad," I agreed. "But writing scripts is what I really want to do."

"A shame."

"You do some writing yourself?"

"Oh, I used to. Short stories, mostly when I was a student at Stanford," she answered. "Nothing ever came of it. Well, good morning, Mr. Denby, and we're pleased that you're feeling better."

"Thank you one and all," I said and returned to my shaving.

While awaiting our arrival in the Super Chief dining car, Groucho sat at his table and whiled away the time by humming a medley of tunes from *The Mikado* and keeping time with his spoon against the leg of the table.

He was midway through "A Wandering Minstrel I," when a portly fellow at the table behind him, after some impressive throat clearing, said, "I beg your pardon, sir, but my wife and I find that quite annoying."

Sitting up straight, Groucho slowly turned. "You and your mate are to be congratulated," he told him. "Myself, I have trouble finding it at all, even with a map."

Frowning, slightly perplexed, the man said, "What I mean is, will you, please, stop?" His wife, a thin greying woman, was also giving Groucho a puzzled look.

"The real thing you should be fretting about is *can* I stop," explained Groucho. "Once, in East Moline, I had a fit of humming that went on for sixteen straight hours. Nothing seemed to halt it, including breathing into a paper sack, drinking water out of the wrong side of the glass, and making a special novena. Finally someone thought of bribery and that turned the trick. Speaking of turning tricks, haven't I met your wife somewhere before or—"

"Good morning, Groucho. Am I interrupting something?" Dian Bowers, after a cautious look around the dining car, had come over to his table and was standing looking down at him.

"Not at all, my dear. I was merely finishing up my morning vituperation exercises." He popped to his feet, gestured at the chair on the opposite side of the table. "Sit down, tell me how you're faring."

The dark-haired actress seated herself. "Well, actually, I'm damned angry," she told him. "I'm hoping you can help me."

"I'd be delighted to, just so long as it doesn't involve any physical effort or anything beyond a modest outlay of cash."

She smiled, very briefly. "I told you that I'm going to attend the opening of my husband's play in New York," she said, glancing once over her shoulder. "It's this Tuesday night and I'd like you to accompany me."

Groucho assumed a demure pose and rolled his eyes somewhat. "Golly, and I was hoping you were going to ask me to the Senior Prom," he said. "But I guess I can escort you to *Make Mine Murder*. Except, of course, I won't be able to wear my new formal."

She leaned forward, lowering her voice. "Manheim's still not too happy about the idea," she confided. "He hasn't said he'll try to stop me, but he and Arneson have been urging me not to go. So I'd feel a lot better if someone I trusted came along with me for moral support."

"I don't, the last time we checked, have any morals, my dear," he said. "However, I'll be happy to see that you get to the opening safely and that no goons, goniffs or producers stop you."

"I'm staying at the Waldorf," Dian said. "And you're at . . . ?"

"The Edison Hotel," he answered. "They named it that because they're hoping to add electricity any day now. Phone me once you've checked in. I'll keep the evening free for you." He drew a cigar out of a side pocket of his umber-colored sports coat, looking directly at the young woman. "Maybe you ought to start thinking seriously about breaking your contract with Manheim. If he's going to keep—"

"It's okay, Groucho. I can, with some help from people like you, handle things," Dian assured him. "And, well, I still think I want to be a success in this business."

He dropped the cigar back into the pocket. "The other evening," he said, "when I stumbled on Arneson and found your beloved producer enjoying an enforced snooze, where were you?"

Her forehead wrinkled. "I was in my bedroom."

"Didn't hear anything, notice anything?"

She sighed. "Oh, you're wondering why I didn't come out to see what all the fuss was about in the corridor," she said. "I don't sleep very well on trains and . . . I took some sleeping pills. I slept through the whole damned incident."

"So did Manheim," said Groucho. "Who do you think made that try at knifing him?"

"Could have been anybody," Dian said, looking away again. "He's not a very likeable man. And it's also possible that the . . ." She let the sentence fade away.

Groucho cupped his ear. "How's that again, my dear?"

The actress shook her head. "Nothing," she said. "Something occurred to me, but then I realized it was foolish."

"I have a whole scrapbook full of foolish notions. Tell me."

"No, really, Groucho. It's not anything important and—oops. I see Arneson looming in the doorway. I'll phone you in Manhattan. And thanks." Hurriedly, she got up and crossed to another table.

Arneson came lumbering in and joined her, after glowering across at Groucho.

Groucho raised his water glass in a toasting gesture. "May you fall off a bridge," he muttered very quietly, smiling falsely.

Turning in his chair, he said to the portly man, "I'm going to start humming again. Is there any special song you'd like to hear?"

Fifteen

We arrived in Chicago later that morning. In the afternoon, after being partially treated to lunch at a nearby delicatessen that Groucho professed to have fond memories of, we boarded the Twentieth Century Limited for New York City.

This streamliner was a bit more sedate in its décor than the Super Chief, going in for grey and silver rather than bold desert colors.

About fifteen minutes out of the station I decided to find a lounge car and get a cup of coffee. Jane chose to stay in our compartment and work on some notes for her next *Hollywood Molly* continuity. So I was roaming a swaying corridor alone when a voice exclaimed, "Frank! Just the man I want to see."

A slim arm reached out through the open doorway of the bedroom I'd been passing and May Sankowitz yanked me inside.

After kissing me enthusiastically on the cheek, she sat me down in a chair and leaned close. "Okay, tell me everything you know."

"Well, it all began when the world was created in the year four-thousand-four B.C. and the—"

"Dope, I mean about what was going on aboard the Super Chief," she said, giving me a poke in the ribs and an impatient look. "I got a hunch I can sell some stories to the news syndicates—in addition to my regular magazine assignment."

"You still with *Hollywood Screen Magazine?*"

"Not only am I still with them, I was promoted to associate managing editor since last we met."

"Which means?"

"Fifty bucks a week more."

May was a small, slim woman getting close to fifty. She was a reddish blonde just now and I'd known her since we both worked for the *Los Angeles Times*. Then she'd run the lonelyhearts column as Dora Dayton. For the past year or more she'd been writing for the movie fan magazine.

"And how come," I asked her, "you're on this train?"

May sighed, closed the toilet, and sat on the padded lid. "Manheim persuaded my nitwit bosses that a blow-by-blow account of his new discovery's arrival in Manhattan would titillate our multitude of moronic readers. So I'm stuck with writing a travel diary—*I Take Manhattan with Dian Bowers*. It means making the last lap of the train ride with the allegedly demure actress and following her hither and yon for her first day in New York City."

"How'd you get to Chicago?"

She pointed a thumb at the ceiling. "Flew."

"Welcome aboard. You can have dinner with Jane and me—and maybe Groucho."

"Skip the sociable stuff, Frank. Tell me about the attempt to murder Manheim." She leaned forward, resting her hands on her knees.

"For some reason," I mentioned, "Hal Arneson is trying to keep the whole business quiet. Might not be a good idea to annoy them by trying to cover—"

"Let me worry about that, dear. Just provide me with some juicy details."

"How'd you hear about it anyway?"

"I know some of the kids in the *Watch Your Step* company and I happened to cross paths with them in Chicago. So?"

I eyed the ceiling for a few seconds. "Okay, and keep in mind that most of what I know is secondhand," I began. "I wasn't a witness to much of anything."

I then gave May a relatively concise account of what had been going on.

When I concluded my narrative, May stood up, smoothed her skirt and nodded. "If you ask me, kid, little Dian Bowers is a definite jinx."

"How so?"

"Well, her hubby had a whole stewpot of bad luck trying to get work out on the coast. Nick Sanantonio got himself gunned down in the street. Now Manheim is attacked while—"

"Whoa, wait. What does that dead gambler have to do with Dian?"

May made an impatient noise, sat down again, crossed her legs. "As I understand it, Dian Bowers had a very hot and heavy little romantic affair with the late Mr. Sanantonio. So much so that Manheim went through the ceiling and ordered his sweet little saint to knock it off or he'd make it extremely tough for all concerned."

"She looks like a very sweet and innocent young—"

"Hey, dummy, she's an actress, remember? Acting innocent isn't that tough," the writer reminded me. "I'm not saying she's a tramp or anything like that, but she hasn't been especially loyal to her estranged husband. I hear, though, that she hasn't given in to Manheim so far."

"Gosh, between you and Johnny Whistler all my boyish beliefs are getting shattered."

May cupped both hands around one knee and leaned back. "Sanantonio was quite a tomcat, especially with ladies in the movies," she said. "For a while, a few months back, Willa Jerome and he were a very hot item."

"She's on this train, too."

"I know, Frank dear, which is why I dropped her name."

I asked, "Any ideas about a motive for trying to stick a knife in Manheim?"

She shrugged. "Too many candidates for the job," she said. "A large percentage of the Hollywood population isn't especially fond of the guy."

"Has to have been somebody who was on the Super Chief."

"Sure, but not necessarily somebody whose name is on the passenger list, Frank," she pointed out. "Like me, somebody could've flown out of LA. Caught up with the train, hopped aboard, made a try for the bastard, and hopped off."

"Maybe," I said.

"Are you and Groucho doing your detective act again?"

"Not anymore, no," I assured her and explained about Manheim's requesting that we lay off.

May said, "The world might be a better place if you guys did forget the whole darn thing and let somebody knock Manheim off."

"Possibly, although I would like to know who conked me on the head."

Her eyes widened. "You didn't mention that before, Frank. Tell me about it."

I told her about it.

As Groucho was about to enter the dining car, with a copy of *Variety* tucked under his arm, a plump woman in a flower-print dress and a fox fur entered the corridor.

She recognized him, gasped, and exclaimed, "Groucho Marx!"

"What a coincidence. That's my name, too."

After taking a deep breath, she told him, "My son wants to be just like you."

"You mean the poor lad wants to be middle-aged, wrinkled, balding, and incontinent?"

"No, no. He wants to be a movie comedian and you're his absolute favorite," she explained. "Why, he worships the ground you walk on."

"Ah, then I'm sorry I walked through the stockyards during the layover in Chicago."

Smiling and frowning at the same time, the plump woman said, "He's seen all the Marx Brothers movies at least three times. And he knows every line in *A Night at the Opera* by heart."

"That's something. Chico never even knew all of his own lines." He prepared to circle the woman and push on into the dining car.

She extracted a sheet of blank hotel stationery from her purse. "Could you sign this for him?"

Groucho accepted the sheet, rested it against the corridor wall, and uncapped his fountain pen. "What's the lad's name?"

"Stanley."

" 'Dear Stanley,' " Groucho said aloud as he wrote, " 'your mother picked my pocket on the Twentieth Century Limited. I'll let it go this time, but if she does it again I suggest you have her carted away. Your humble servant, Elihu Root (a.k.a. Groucho Marx).' "

As he handed the sheet of paper back to her, she said, "You're a funny man, Mr. Marx."

"One of us has to be and, alas, the task fell to me." He entered the dining car.

Jane and I were already there, seated at a table midway along.

"He looks gloomy," observed my wife as Groucho came slouching toward us.

"He always looks gloomy. Most great clowns are tragic figures at—"

"I bet it has something to do with that *Variety* he's clutching."

"Greetings, my children." Groucho seated himself across from us, placed the tabloid on the table in front of him. "Who would you say, off-hand, is the greatest interpreter of Gilbert and Sullivan in the entire civilized world?"

"Martyn Green?" suggested Jane.

"Let me rephrase the question," he said. "Who's the world's greatest interpreter of Gilbert and Sullivan who happens to be sitting at this table with you?"

"You?" she asked.

"Right the first time." Groucho turned to an inside page of the show business paper. "Someone left this periodical in the observation car and, borrowing it, I discover therein the news that there have already been not one but two versions of *The Mikado* on Broadway this year."

"Sure, *The Swing Mikado* and *The Hot Mikado*," said Jane. "Both flopped, so they won't be competing with you."

"Even so, it plants the notion in the public mind that *The Mikado* is a clinker," complained Groucho. "They'll think it's another *Room Service*."

"You're giving them the tried-and-true version," I pointed out. "Not a swing adaptation."

"People will flock to see you," predicted Jane. "Don't fret."

"Well, I have to admit I am a potentially fabled performer in the Gilbert and Sullivan area," he said with obvious false modesty. "Why, not since the glorious days when D'Oyly Carte first staged *The Mikado*—or even earlier, when they put the D'Oyly Carte before the horse—has anyone performed Gilbert and Sullivan the way I do."

"All too true," acknowledged Jane.

He closed the tabloid. "Let's just hope that Olsen and Johnson don't decide to do their version," he said and picked up his menu card.

"I found out something interesting about the case," I told him.

"We don't have a case, Watson," he reminded. "You are but a humble radio writer and I am a roving Savoyard. We are not in the gumshoe trade at the moment."

"You ought" put in Jane, "to hear this anyway, Groucho."

"Very well, my boy, you may tell me. But please don't use that annoying Swedish accent you've been affecting of late."

Nodding, I filled him in on what I'd found out from May Sankowitz about the romances the late Nick Sanantonio had allegedly carried on with Dian Bowers and Willa Jerome. I concluded, "I'm not exactly sure it has a damn thing to do with what happened to Manheim and Arneson. But it is sort of interesting."

"Like the flowers that bloom in the spring, Rollo, it probably has nothing to do with the case." Leaning back in his chair, Groucho took a cigar out of his coat pocket. "Big-time gamblers tend to be irresistible to women. Chico's the same way. Whereas myself, who limits his activities in that area to bingo and pitching pennies, am notably unlucky in love."

"Did you know about Dian and Sanantonio?" Jane asked him.

He shook his head. "I hadn't the faintest scintilla of a notion," he admitted. "Matter of fact, up until last Tuesday I didn't even know what a scintilla was." Unwrapping the cigar, he lit it. "But, since we no longer have any interest in this particular mess, I'm not going to worry my pretty little head about who's doing what to whom." He exhaled smoke. "I advise you two cherubs to do the same."

The streamliner was clacking through the night and we were in the vicinity of Cleveland. From the lower bunk Jane said, "I've been thinking."

"No good will come of it." Up in my berth I'd been reading the new issue of *Black Mask* I'd picked up at a newsstand in the Chicago railroad station. I estimated I was less than five minutes from dozing off.

"About that newest *Hollywood Molly* radio show synopsis you cooked up this afternoon, Frank."

"You want to upgrade your rating from 'okay' to 'super terrific'? "

Jane hesitated, then said, "When it comes to writing radio shows, you're the expert."

"Absolutely true, yes. But?"

"Well, I've done all my own writing on the comic strip," she continued. "Not that you haven't been a great help as an editor on the continuities, obviously, and you've helped me work out some plot snags and polish dialogue now and then."

"You forgot to mention that I'm a whiz when it comes to punctuation."

"Hey, you're starting to sound like you're getting miffed up there."

"I am not miffed," I assured her from my upper bed.

"All the other sample story lines we've worked out to present to the radio people in New York are just fine," Jane said. "But this new one of yours . . . well, it just doesn't suit Molly."

"You sound like some movie studio executive."

"See, you *are* miffed."

"Nope, I'm disheartened to realize I married a woman who talks like an associate producer."

"Whenever you get angry you try to insult me and—"

"Calling you an associate producer isn't an especially vicious—"

"You always get this way. Really, Frank, a little harmless criticism and you blow up like a—"

"What harmless criticism? What I'm hearing is that my ideas stink."

"I never said that."

"Just because I happen to be between radio or movie assignments, doesn't mean I can't come up with a—"

"Let me, please, get to my point before you start moaning and groaning up there."

"Oh, now the fact that I have, once again, sacrificed my comfort to try to sleep in this lofty perch so that you can bask in the comfort of the lower—"

"All I'm trying to tell you is that I don't want to have a murder-mystery plot on the *Hollywood Molly* radio show."

I said, "You thought the idea was great this afternoon."

"I thought it was okay. After thinking it over, I decided that—"

"Having Molly's actress pal, Vicky Fairweather, fall in love with a big-time Los Angeles gambler is a good notion, Jane," I insisted. "Plus which, it's topical. Then when the gangster gets killed, Molly's friend is accused of murder and she has to play detective so—"

"Don't tell me the whole stupid idea over again, if you don't mind."

"Stupid, huh? I wrote radio scripts for Groucho Marx for two years, but I'm stupid. I sold a screwball movie script to—"

"Groucho's standards and mine aren't the same," my wife pointed out from below. "I'd prefer not to have Molly acting like an idiot and trying to solve murder cases on my radio show."

I took a deep breath in and out. "Write your own damn show then," I told her. I turned off my light and maintained a hurt silence.

The Twentieth Century Limited rushed on through the night.

After about fifteen minutes Jane said, "Frank?"

"Yeah?"

"I suppose one murder wouldn't hurt."

"No, you're probably right. It doesn't fit with Molly."

Jane said, "We can talk about it tomorrow. Good night."

"Good night."

Sixteen

Early on Monday morning Groucho was leaving the lounge car, where he'd sung "Lydia the Tattooed Lady" twice, signed three autograph albums, and insulted two Manhattan-bound stockbrokers, when he encountered Dr. Dowling in the gently rocking corridor of the streamliner.

The plump personal physician of Willa Jerome was pale and slightly rumpled, but close to sober. "I'm not sure we've met, Mr. Marx," he said, halting in Groucho's path.

"If we'd met it would be indelibly etched in your memory, sir," Groucho assured him. "A female equestrian, for example, who met me, only briefly, in Bangor, Maine, in the spring of nineteen-twenty-six, has never been able to forget the occasion and on the anniversary each year she puts a bouquet of yellow roses on the spot. This is extremely difficult, since the spot in question happens to be beneath a—"

"What I meant was—I've been pretty much under the weather all the way from Los Angeles and my memory is a little fuzzy in spots," he explained. "I'm Dr. Daniel Dowling, traveling with Willa Jerome's party."

"Ah, I wasn't aware she brought a party along. I wonder why I wasn't invited."

Dowling smiled, a bit ruefully. "I heard that your friend Mr. Denby was injured. Is he all right now?"

"Yes, Frank's fine. He's sitting up and taking nourishment," Groucho answered. "He's also taken the purse of a little old lady who's traveling to Manhattan to open a drive-in seraglio."

Dowling said, "I hear, too, that you and Denby have been investigating what happened to Manheim on the Super Chief."

"Very briefly." Groucho took out a cigar. "We've since retired from the case."

"What's your theory as to what went on?"

"I wasn't on the job long enough to come up with a full-fledged theory."

"So you don't suspect anyone in particular?"

Groucho elevated his left eyebrow. "Do you?"

"No, not at all," said Dr. Dowling. "It's only that I was, naturally, curious. That sort of thing is unusual on a trip east."

"It rarely even happens on a trip west, for that matter."

Dowling chuckled without much enthusiasm. "Well, it's been pleasant to meet you, Mr. Marx," he said. "Perhaps we'll meet again in New York."

"Worse things have happened," observed Groucho, moving on.

Our train pulled into Grand Central Station at a few minutes shy of 10:00 A.M. By a few minutes after, Jane and I were following a Red Cap and our assorted baggage along the strip of red carpet that the New York Central System spreads out for passengers disembarking from the Twentieth Century Limited. According to the promotional handout, the piece of broadloom we were treading on was exactly 260 feet long.

Groucho, guitar case swinging at his side, was slouching along with us toward the gate leading to the main concourse. "Why, may I ask," he said, "are all these other travelers traipsing on *my* carpeting?"

"The red carpet treatment is for everybody," said Jane.

His eyebrows rose. "You mean, Brünhilde, that this isn't part of the exclusive welcome that Mayor LaGuardia has arranged to commemorate my advent in Manhattan?"

"Seems not."

Groucho sighed. "On previous visits I was treated like royalty," he said. "Of course, the royalty they treated me like was Mad King Ludwig of Bavaria, but even so it was heartwarming."

"The least you would expect," said Jane sympathetically, "is the key to the city."

"On my last sojourn LaGuardia did give me the key to the city. Not *this* city, admittedly, yet the thought was there."

Jane noticed that I was frowning at the crowd of recent passengers that was marching up ahead of us. "Something wrong?" she inquired.

"I just noticed May Sankowitz walking up there about twenty or so people ahead of us," I said. "Looks like Len Cowan, the dancer, is with her."

Stretching up, Groucho peered ahead. "He is, Rollo," he confirmed. "Which is deuced odd, since the entire *Step Right Up* troupe was supposed to have remained in Chicago."

"Maybe he isn't through heckling Manheim."

Glancing around, Jane said, "I don't see any sign of Manheim or his protégée."

"They're remaining aboard the train until the peasantry has withdrawn," explained Groucho. "Then they're holding a small press conference out under the clock." He shook his head forlornly. "Ah, I well remember when I was the darling of the newspapers and reporters flocked to interview me. I was also, until they got a closer look at me, the Sweetheart of Sigma Chi and for good measure the—"

"Julius Marx," exclaimed a somewhat nasal voice. "Welcome to the world's largest flea market, sometimes known as Manhattan."

An extremely dapper man of about forty, grey haired, grey suited, and wearing a snap-brim grey fedora, was hurrying along the train platform toward us.

"Leo, companion of my childhood," said Groucho.

"It's Leo Haskell," Jane told me quietly as the two men embraced.

"Who?"

"Haskell, the poor man's Walter Winchell," she elaborated. "He writes the *Broadway Beat* column for the *New York Daily Tab*."

"Oh, that Haskell."

"I'm touched," Groucho was saying, "that you came to greet me, Leo, and welcome me to—"

"To be honest, Groucho, I'm here to interview this week's hot cinemaiden," the Broadway columnist told him. "Dian Bowers they call her out in Tinselvania. But, listen, I can always use an inch about you. What's this I hear about you walking the planks on Broadway again, in some Japaretta?"

"I'll be doing *The Mikado* at the—"

"Word is that the latest celluloid opus you and your brothers have perpetrated is a massive stinkeroo of the first order. True or false, Groucho?"

"It is a wee bit fragrant, Leo, but—"

"And what the heck's the lowdown on Manheim? Did somebody really try to ventilate his clockwork en route to the Apple? Did they attempt to close his drapes for good or—"

"Whoa. Give me a chance to read the subtitles under your dialogue, Leo."

"Whoops, there's Willa Jerome, the lithesome Limey lass, and her entourage coming our way," said Haskell, looking beyond Groucho. "I'll be ankling, Groucho. Give me a jingle." He left us.

We started walking again. "That was Leo Haskell," said Groucho.

"So we gathered," I said.

"In my youth, which is now officially known as the Dark Ages, my brothers and I shared several vaudeville bills with Leo. He was a mere hoofer in those days and hadn't yet discovered his God-given ability to mangle the English language and peer through keyholes."

Jane and I parted with Groucho in front of the terminal and in less than a half hour we were in our hotel suite on Central Park South.

Wearing her slip and a candy-stripe blouse, Jane was sitting cross-legged on the love seat in the living room of our suite at the St. Norbert Hotel. She had a copy of the latest *New Yorker* open on her lap and was studying the *Goings-On About Town* section.

I was standing by a high, wide window and gazing down at the afternoon Central Park far below.

"How about Buddy Ebsen?" asked Jane.

"In what context?"

"As a dancer starring in this new musical *Yokel Boy*. We could see if we can get tickets for that or—"

The phone rang again.

I answered it. "Yeah?"

"Is this Miss Danner's secretary?" inquired a very polite female voice.

"Actually I'm one of her valets," I said. "But I can convey a message."

"This is Mr. Diggs' secretary at Empire Features Syndicate," she said. "Might I speak to her?"

"Sure. Hold on."

Jane untangled herself from the love seat and I handed her the receiver. "Yes, hello," she said. "Oh, certainly. We like the suite very much and I want to thank you all for arranging it for us. Tomorrow afternoon?" She put her hand over the mouthpiece. "Tomorrow at two o'clock for our first meeting at the syndicate okay by you?"

I was back at the window watching Central Park South. "I'm only a humble lackey, mum. Mine is not to reason why, mine—"

"Yes, that'll be fine," she told the phone, thumbing her nose at me. "Oh, really? Yes, that would be swell. I'll get back to you on that, Miss Spaulding. Fine. Good-bye now." Hanging up, Jane returned to her chair. "Miss Spaulding, who's the private secretary of the syndicate president, says they can get us whatever theater tickets we might want."

"Can they give us a roll of nickels to use at the Automat, too?"

Jane stood up again, eyeing me. "Boy, you're sure being a sourpuss," she observed. "Are you still upset because my syndicate is treating us to this hotel suite and all the—"

"I guess I am, yeah. Freeloading off Empire Features isn't exactly the way I like to—"

"Well, I think it's swell," she said, hands on hips. "And, Frank, this is something I earned. Me, with very little help from anybody else. The way I see our marriage—sometimes you earn the money, sometimes I do, most times we both do. So don't begrudge me the times when I'm doing terrific in my chosen profession, huh?"

I sulked for about thirty seconds, then thought better of it. "Okay, sorry," I said. "Won't happen again."

She sat, retrieved the magazine. "Or would you rather see Carmen Miranda?"

"Is she the one who wears bananas on her head?"

"She also sings and she's in a show called *The Streets of Paris*. We could see if we can get tickets to that," said Jane. "There's also a new comedy team called Lou Costello and Bud Abbott in that one."

"Used to be if you wore bananas on your head, they locked you up someplace."

"Not if you're from Brazil."

"I'm still not clear as to what a Brazilian Bombshell is doing on the streets of Paris."

"We could go to the darn show and find out, Frank."

"Let's go to both of them, Ebsen and Carmen Miranda," I suggested. "Not concurrently, but on—"

The telephone rang again.

Seventeen

The murder didn't take place until that Tuesday night.

Groucho, as he later told me, had spent most of the afternoon at a rehearsal hall down in the West 30s working on *The Mikado*. Earlier he'd had lunch with George S. Kaufman and Monty Woolley at the Algonquin. Kaufman, with Moss Hart, had written *The Man Who Came to Dinner* and Woolley was starring in it at the Music Box. "Why people will pay good money to see a fellow portray a hairy Alec Woollcott is beyond me," Groucho had informed them.

At a little after seven that evening, dressed in a conservative dark suit, Groucho was slouching unobtrusively along Broadway in the theatrical district. Under his breath he was singing lines from *The Mikado*. "Behold the Lord High Executioner. A person of noble rank and title."

A plump middle-aged woman emerged from a coffee shop, glanced at him, then gasped. "I know who you are," she said.

Groucho halted. "Well, quick, tell me. I'm simply dying to know."

"You're George S. Kaufman, aren't you?"

He leaned closer, confiding, "Right you are, madam. I am indeed the renowned playwright and podiatrist."

"We laughed all through *The Man Who Came to Dinner*. Last week, my husband and I."

"Yes, and I can tell you there were a lot of complaints about the pair of you. Here I pen a somber tragedy and you and your spouse go tittering all over the place and spoiling it for everybody."

After eyeing him for a few seconds, she giggled. "You're pulling my leg, Mr. Kaufman."

Groucho rolled his eyes, shook his head. "I pass. I won't respond to such obvious bait."

"Tell me, what's your next play going to be? I hear rumors that you and Mr. Hart have a new—"

"I've made up my mind to try a comedy this time," he informed her. "It will be based on the life of the funniest man in America. A humble fellow named Groucho Marx."

"Oh, he's not all that funny," she said, nose wrinkling. "If you want to see somebody who's really funny, go catch Bobby Clark in *The Streets of Paris*."

"By Jove," he said, moving along, "I believe I'll do that at once."

A few moments later he entered Alfie's Pub, a narrow shadowy little bar just off Broadway. He stood for a moment near the paneled door. Then he spotted Dian Bowers sitting by herself in a booth.

He made his way over to her, bowed, kissed her hand, and sat opposite. "You're looking a mite peaked, my child. Is all well?"

"To be honest, Groucho," said the actress, "not much is well at all. Manheim and Arneson have been at me off and on all day not to go to the opening of Jim's play tonight." She sighed quietly. "Matter of fact, I had to sneak out of the hotel to come over here and meet you."

"Women who rendezvous with me often have to sneak and slink," he said. "You really, however, have to tell Manheim that his overly paternal attitudes toward you are—"

"And I also think he's got somebody shadowing me."

Groucho glanced around the moderately crowded bar. "Somebody other than Arneson?"

"It's okay, I think I ditched the guy," she said. "A seedy fellow, some sort of private investigator, I'd guess."

"How big is he?"

"Not more than five foot four or so."

"In that case I'm prepared to thrash the fellow should he cause you any trouble," volunteered Groucho. "And since I recently invented a thrashing machine, I'll be—"

"I'm really not too happy about the way things are going, Groucho."

"You can wear a veil and nobody will know I'm your escort, my dear."

"I mean, I'm so damned tired of being told what I can and can't do, who I can see, where I can go," she said forlornly. "I'm tired of the whole business."

"After *Saint Joan* opens, kiddo, you'll be a star and you can tell everybody where to get off," he said. "Of course, you can also do that if you're a bus driver and that's a lot less trying."

Dian smiled. "I'm sorry I'm in such a gloomy mood," she said. "Tell me what you've been up to."

"The worst thing that's happened all day is that I was accused of being George S. Kaufman."

"Come to think of it, Groucho, you do look a little bit like him."

"Only below the waist," he said.

She reached across to pat his hand. "Would you like something to drink before we head for the Coronet Theatre?"

"I would," replied Groucho. "But I don't see Ovaltine on the menu."

The tickets Bill Washburn had left for his estranged wife at the box office were for seats in the third row of the orchestra section.

A very stylishly dressed matron in the seat behind Groucho said to her handsome escort, "Look, dear, isn't that the theater critic George Jean Nathan over there on the aisle?"

"Looks a good deal like him, Iris."

Groucho turned, resting his elbow on the back of his seat. "Actually, folks, that's Nathan Jean George, his cousin."

"I'll thank you not to intrude on a private conversation, sir," admonished the handsome escort.

"And I'll thank you not to continue to babble once the play starts," Groucho said. "It annoys me extremely when people talk while I'm trying to eat peanut brittle and clip my toenails."

"You're a first-class boor," said the woman.

"It's too late to try to flatter me now."

Dian touched Groucho's arm, saying quietly, "This isn't my opening night, but I sure feel nervous and uneasy."

"Perhaps you still identify with your husband," he suggested.

"I suppose I do."

"Could be you still like the guy."

She said, "Yes, I think so."

Groucho glanced back at the couple behind them. "Don't look now, folks, but Gene Tunney, Gene Tierney, King George, and Nathan Delicatessen just came in and sat on George Jean Nathan's lap."

They both ignored him.

About ten minutes later the houselights dimmed and the curtain rose on the first act of *Make Mine Murder*. It was a comedy mystery, pretty much in *The Cat and the Canary* tradition. The opening scenes took place in a gloomy Long Island mansion during a thunderstorm. An assortment of lively, and mostly suspicious, characters were gathering for the midnight reading of a will.

The actress who was taking the part of the granddaughter of the deceased eccentric millionaire was Elena Styverson, who'd been playing ingenues on Broadway for nearly a decade now. Her first entrance drew enthusiastic applause from the audience. Bill Washburn, a lean dark-haired young man, had the part of Jake Scanlon, a wisecracking reporter for a New York tabloid. He'd barged into the mansion, hoping for a story about the dead man's allegedly strange will. When he initially stepped onto the stage, there wasn't much in the way of applause, except from Dian and Groucho.

Pringle, the crotchety old lawyer who knew the secret of the will, vanished mysteriously at the end of the second scene. In the third, the reporter and the granddaughter, who'd formed a somewhat bickering team, decided to hunt for the old man. The veteran actor Andrew Truett was playing the lawyer.

When they were alone in the living room, with lightning flashing and thunder booming outside in the stormy night, Elena Styverson said, "You know, Mr. Scanlon, in the movies they always—"

"Hey, kid, you can call me Jake. All my friends do."

She smiled, moving toward a closet door. "Okay, Jake."

"And you were saying, sweetheart?"

"Oh, that in the movies they always find missing people stowed in the closet."

Washburn laughed, pushing his hat brim up. "That's only in the movies."

"Even so, Mr.—I mean, Jake. Even so, we'd better look and make sure Mr. Pringle hasn't gotten in there somehow."

Laughing, Washburn strode to the closet door and took hold of the knob and turned it. "Come out of there, Pringle, old boy."

He yanked the door open.

A body fell out and slammed onto the Persian carpet with an echoing thud.

Elena Styverson screamed.

Washburn started to put an arm around her, then stepped back and said, "Holy Christ, that's not a dummy."

Dian, exhaling sharply, gripped Groucho's arm. "My god, it's Manheim."

"That it is," he agreed. "And this time it looks like he's really dead."

Eighteen

About the same time that Daniel Manheim's body was making its Broadway debut, I was contemplating doing violence to an executive of the Empire Feature Syndicate.

This was in the East 50s at a new and currently fashionable nightclub called El Pobrecito. It was a large black-and-white place, something like the huge fictitious hot spots you see in Fred Astaire–Ginger Rogers musicals. Jane and I had been taken there by the president of her newspaper syndicate and joined by the syndicate sales manager and an advertising agency executive who was going to handle producing our *Hollywood Molly* radio show.

The Empire Feature Syndicate sales manager was a tall, wide guy named Dobbs Walling. He was good-looking, in his middle thirties, and at the moment out on the glistening black dance floor doing, I think, a samba with my wife to the rhythms of José Fayal and his Brazilian Bunch.

Walling had brought along a pretty brunette debutante named Brenda. She was sitting on the other side of Jane's empty chair. Leaning toward me, she said, "He dances that way with everybody. Don't let it bother you."

"I was just worrying that the referee would charge him with a foul," I said.

Smiling very faintly, she said, "Dobbs is harmless, really." She took a silver cigarette case out of her purse. "Like one?"

"Don't smoke, thanks."

"You're the writer, aren't you?"

"Writer and irate husband, yeah."

She selected a cork-tip cigarette and I fished a book of matches out of my coat pocket to light it. "Trocadero, huh?" she said, glancing at the matchbook. "God, I haven't been out to the Coast since April."

I was back to watching the husky Walling dance with my wife. "Oh, so?"

Ralph Diggs, a portly man in his middle fifties who was president of EFS, was sitting directly across from me. "I believe that was a terrific preliminary meeting we had this afternoon, Frank," he said. "I really liked the ideas you and Janey have cooked up for our radio show. So did Wally."

I wasn't exactly clear as to who Wally was, but I said, "Well, that's gratifying to—"

"Have you given any more thought to the kid brother?" asked Milt Banion, who was with the McKay and Forman advertising outfit.

"Which kid brother?" I inquired.

"Our thinking at the agency is that Molly needs a cute kid brother. Somewhat like the one in that other comic strip . . ."

Ella Cinders," supplied Diggs. "But we're not convinced that's necessary, Milt."

"Leon Janney would be great as her kid brother." Banion was a lean blonde man with a thin blonde moustache. "He's available. We could call the kid something like Blackie."

"That's Ella Cinders's brother," Diggs pointed out.

"It could be Curly or Buster or Freckles."

"There's a Freckles in somebody else's strip, Milt."

"Okay, I'll leave it to creative minds of the likes of Fred here. He and Janey can—"

"Frank and Jane," I corrected. "And we don't think it's too smart to change the cast of characters just—"

"Is there a Mr. Dumpty at the table?" Our waiter had appeared, carrying a white plug-in telephone.

"No such person," said Banion. "Tell them Mr. Dumpty had a great fall and—"

"Could that be Mr. Denby?" I inquired.

"Might just be," decided the waiter. "There's a call for you from somebody claiming to be Groucho Marx."

"Yes, it's a sad case," I said. "He frequently claims to be Groucho Marx. I'll take the call."

"Who is he really?" asked Brenda.

"Groucho Marx." I picked up the receiver. "Are you there? Frank Dumpty here."

"I hesitated over interrupting your company picnic, Rollo," said Groucho. "But a little something has come up."

"Such as?"

"Manheim has been murdered."

"Jesus. Where?"

"As the finale of the first act of *Make Mine Murder,*" he answered. "If you can see your way clear to trotting over here to the Coronet Theatre, I've arranged with the minions of the law to let you sneak in backstage."

"How the hell did you arrange that?"

"I happen to know one of these particular minions."

"And how'd you track me to this bistro?"

"By using mystical powers that I picked up years ago in the Orient. Unfortunately, I also picked up an annoying rash in the vicinity of my . . . but plenty of time to chat about that when you arrive here at the scene of the crime."

"You seem to be implying that we may be back in business."

"I am, kiddo," Groucho replied. "The main reason being that I've a hunch they're going to try to pin the murder on Dian's husband, Bill Washburn. See you soon." He hung up.

Jane returned to her chair just as I put down the phone. Then she leaned back, frowning. "What's wrong?" she asked, touching my hand.

"Oh, it's just one of those nagging bouts of jealous rage I suffer from," I confided in a very low voice. "I don't know, every time I see a total stranger clutching your backside, I get—"

"Walling isn't a *total* stranger," she said, smiling. "But, hey, what I meant was—who just phoned you?"

"Groucho. Seems somebody's killed Manheim over at the Coronet Theatre," I said. "Apparently during the damn play."

"And Groucho is on the case already and wants you to join him?"

"Yeah," I answered, nodding. "I'd better get over there. You can stay here if you want."

"And have to grapple with Walling again?" she said. "No. I'll tag along with you. If you don't mind?"

"Not at all."

Nineteen

As the curtain came rushing down, Dian stood and grabbed her wrap from the back of the theater seat. "I've got to get backstage," she said.

Groucho, as he later told me, popped to his feet. "I'll escort you, my child," he offered.

They hurried along the aisle to one of the doors that led backstage.

The audience, starting to get over its shock, was murmuring, talking, shifting in its seats.

Taking hold of the young actress's arm, Groucho guided her up the short, narrow staircase and through the doorway.

There was considerable noise and movement back there. It was still fairly dark, but as they started across the bare boards, overhead lights blossomed.

A husky stagehand noticed them and came striding over. "Stay out in the house, folks, where you belong," he ordered in his raspy voice. "No kibitzing, okay?"

Dian said, "I'm Bill Washburn's wife."

The big man took a step nearer. "Oh, yeah, I read about you in the *News* yesterday," he said. "I think Bill's still out on the stage." He frowned at Groucho. "And you are, buddy?"

"I'm their spiritual advisor," he explained, following Dian.

The stage was bright-lit now and a tall thin man in his shirtsleeves was on one knee beside the dead producer's body. "Dead as they come," he announced, standing up. "Looks like he was stabbed. No sign of a knife, though."

"Bill," said Dian quietly.

The young actor, pale under his stage makeup, was standing in about the same spot where he'd been when the curtain dropped. He was staring down at Manheim.

Elena Styverson was sitting over on a paisley-pattern love seat, hugging herself and shivering slightly. "Bill, it's your ex," she called out.

He looked up, saw Dian, and, smiling briefly, came hurrying over to her. "Nancy, do you have an idea what the hell's been going on?"

She frowned in the direction of the nearby seated actress. "I'm not his ex, by the way," she said. "We're still married." She put her arms around her husband, hugged him, and then stepped back. "I don't know a damn thing, Bill. What was Manheim doing here at all?"

"Oh, that part I know," he told his wife. "He came to threaten me."

"What do you mean?"

Groucho had eased closer to the couple. "Don't mind me, young folks," he said. "I'll simply park here and eavesdrop."

"Bill, this is Groucho Marx," Dian said.

"Sorry I didn't recognize you, Groucho. You usually have a moustache."

"Yes, but now that my mind's failing, I often come out without it," he explained. "Go on about what Manheim was up to."

"Well, as you probably know, he was extremely protective of Nancy—excuse me, of Dian Bowers," he said. "He came barging into my dressing room about ten minutes before my entrance cue and started yelling at me."

"Suggesting that you stay away from your wife?"

"Exactly, yeah. He told me that he knew I'd invited her to the opening performance tonight," said Washburn. "That I was going to ruin her career if I didn't give her up completely and—"

"I know," cut in Dian. "I've been trying to explain to him that being his bright new discovery didn't mean I was his indentured slave."

Groucho was glancing over at the dead movie producer, who was spread out facedown on the library carpet. "Couple of cuts and bruises on what you can see of Manheim's cheek," he observed. "Seems unlikely he did that when he fell."

Washburn shook his head. "No, I did that," he admitted. "He tried to take a poke at me and . . . well, I slugged the bastard a few times."

"And then?"

"They called me to go on," answered the actor. "So I left Manheim sitting, groggy, in the armchair in my dressing room."

"You never saw him again until he came tumbling out of the closet?"

"That's right, Groucho," said Washburn, nodding. "See, Andy Truett doesn't actually do the fall out of the closet. It's supposed to be a realistic-looking dummy." He pointed a thumb at the open closet door. "Thing is rigged to come toppling out when I yank the door open. Then just before the Act Two curtain rises, Andy comes out and takes the dummy's place. Saves a lot of wear and tear on the old boy."

"Any idea how Manheim came to replace the dummy?

Washburn said, "Nope, not a one."

The gaunt man said, "I noticed the dummy lying behind the flat. That's where whoever tossed it when they replaced it with this guy."

"Anybody see that happen?"

"Nobody's mentioned it as yet, but things are still pretty confused around here." He held out his hand. "I'm Peter Goodwin, by the way, the stage manager."

"Pleased to meet you," Groucho said. "I'm merely an old busybody who's taking an interest in this business."

"I saw you and your brothers in *I'll Say She Is* when I was a kid," said Goodwin. "You were terrific."

"I used to be, yes," said Groucho. "Where's this Andy who plays Lawyer Pringle?"

"Probably snoozing in his dressing room," answered Washburn. "That's what he did during our last couple of dress rehearsals."

"And who would've—"

"Would you folks mind if I took over and asked some questions?" A middle-sized, dark-haired man in a rumpled grey suit had stepped onto the stage and was striding toward them. "I'm Lieutenant Lewin, New York City Police."

Groucho frowned. "About ten years ago weren't you the patrolman Herb Lewin whose beat was the theater district?"

The plainclothes policeman looked more closely at Groucho. "By gosh, Groucho Marx," he said. "I didn't recognize you right off without your moustache."

After touching his upper lip, Groucho shook hands with the cop. "All the public opinion polls seem to agree on that point," he said.

Lewin said, "The rest of my crew will be here in a minute or so. I'd appreciate it if all of you got off the stage and waited for me in the wings." He moved closer to Groucho. "I hear you've been solving mysteries out in Hollywood, playing detective."

"Actually, Herb, I've mostly been playing Old Maid and Gin Rummy."

"And you don't intend to poke around in this case?"

Groucho eyed the catwalks high above the stage. "Well, if you don't mind," he said, "I might do a wee bit of poking."

The body was being carried out of the backstage entrance on a stretcher as we arrived at the Coronet. Three photographers and four reporters were already in the alley, where they'd been working at trying to persuade the two uniformed policemen on duty there to allow them inside the theater.

They went scattering backwards now, turning and following the stretcher. The photographers started to shoot pictures of Manheim's corpse as it was being hauled toward the waiting ambulance.

Jane and I approached one of the cops, a large heavyset guy. "I'm Frank Denby," I said.

"Are you now? And so what?"

My wife smiled at him. "We're wanted inside and we were told we'd be admitted to—"

"Oh, you must be Jane Danner," he said. "I read *Hollywood Molly* every blessed day in the *Sun*. And this lad with you is who exactly?"

"My current husband," she explained, taking hold of my arm.

The policeman nodded. "Lieutenant Lewin did mention you'd be dropping by, Miss Danner," he acknowledged. "You and this fellow can go right in, but, and this is straight from the lieutenant, be sure you don't get in the way."

"We'll be very unobtrusive," she promised as we climbed the three concrete steps to enter the backstage area.

There were several plainclothes officers in the theater, including a forensic crew that was prowling out on stage.

"There he is," I said, spotting Groucho standing by himself over in front of a closed dressing room door. Both his hands were behind his back and he had an unlit cigar grasped in his teeth. "You seem to be lost in thought, Groucho."

"Well, that's better than being lost in the Himalayas," he answered. "And warmer, too." He executed a slouching, flat-footed skating motion and caught Jane's hand. After kissing it with appropriate sound effects, he told her, "Ah, it's a distinct pleasure to see you once again, Miss Jane. You're looking stunning this evening."

"I'm aware of that, yes," she said. "In fact, I paused to stun a few passersby on the way over here, which is why we're a little late."

Groucho gave me a sad look, shaking his head ruefully. "I suppose, Rollo, it's too late to have your marriage annulled?"

"Yeah, because I foolishly went ahead and consummated it already," I replied. "How was Manheim killed?"

"Very dramatically," he said. "He was part of the play and provided, quite probably, one of the best first act curtains in dramatic history.

Selznick, Zanuck, and DeMille will have to go some to depart this world as flamboyantly as did Daniel Manheim." Groucho then outlined to us what had happened during the performance of *Make Mine Murder*.

"Was he stabbed?" I asked when he concluded the account.

Groucho nodded. "Three times, near the heart," he answered. "Very forceful blows."

"Ruling out a woman?"

"Not if she's an athletic type."

Jane asked him, "How come you have details about the wounds and such?"

"Firstly, I am a brilliant observer," he said, holding up his right hand and ticking off a finger. "Secondly, I am a crackerjack detective. And, most important of all, I know Lieutenant Herb Lewin, who's in charge of this investigation, and he told me."

"You're getting cooperation from the police?" I said, surprised.

"We all knew Lewin. He was a pal of ours, back when he was a beat cop here in Manhattan and we were the toast of Broadway," he explained. "Or rather, Harpo, Chico, and Zeppo were the toast and I was the marmalade."

I noticed that Bill Washburn's name was on the placard tacked to the dressing room door. "You told me Washburn was a possible suspect."

Taking my arm and making a come-along gesture toward Jane, he escorted us over to the vicinity of an old humpback prop trunk. Perching on it, Groucho said, "I don't suspect the lad, but Herb Lewin, I'm pretty sure, does."

"Seems unlikely Washburn would murder somebody and hide him on the set of his own darn play," observed Jane.

"My feelings exactly, Nurse Jane," agreed Groucho. "But I'm not a Manhattan minion of the law. And, we must admit, Washburn and Manheim had a conspicuous row in his dressing room just before Washburn went on stage. Further—which didn't please the cops at all—Washburn admits punching our defunct producer. The chaps made considerable noise, which was heard by all and sundry. Including Our Gal Sundry."

"People heard the fracas," I said, "but nobody saw who switched Manheim's body with the dummy?"

"That brings up another interesting point," said Groucho, taking his unlit cigar from his mouth and holding it like a pointer. "It was dark backstage and, because of the aforementioned thunderstorm effects, noisy and distracting. The stagehand who is usually stationed near the backside of the closet door to facilitate the dummy's safe passage fell asleep on the job."

"With some help?" I asked.

"Exactly, Rollo. Somebody bopped him on the coco with the proverbial sap."

"What it sounds like to me," I said, "is the same person who tried for Manheim on the Super Chief. *His* favorite tools included a blackjack and a knife."

"And that would rule out Washburn, since he's been rehearsing this storm-tossed melodrama right here in New York City for over a week and hasn't been aboard even so much as a subway."

Jane suggested, "So maybe you're worrying over nothing, Groucho. It's unlikely the police will—"

The door of Washburn's dressing room snapped open and a middle-sized, dark-haired plainclothes cop came striding out. "We found the weapon, Groucho," he said, holding up a handkerchief-wrapped knife.

Twenty

Just as the police were escorting Bill Washburn out of the theater for further questioning downtown, a very agitated Hal Arneson came pushing his way backstage.

When he recognized the actor, Arneson made a lunge in his direction. "You son of a bitch, you killed Manheim," he accused loudly, attempting to take a swing at him.

One of Lieutenant Lewin's men caught the husky publicity man's arm, tugging him off balance and back. "That's enough, buddy."

Lewin had been standing nearby, talking to Groucho, me, and Jane. "Who's this guy?" he asked us.

"Hal Arneson," I answered. "He's Manheim's flack, troubleshooter, and bodyguard."

"He didn't do too well on that last chore," observed the cop.

"You had it all worked out, huh?" the angry Arneson was shouting. "Decoy me to goddamn Greenwich Village and then lure Manheim here so you could murder him."

"You're nuts," said Washburn. "I didn't have a damn thing to do with—"

"Suppose you talk to me, Mr. Arneson?" the lieutenant said, moving closer to the group. "I'm Lieutenant Lewin, New York Police."

We followed.

"This bastard," said Arneson, breathing through his open mouth, "left a phony message for me at our hotel. It said that Dian wasn't coming here to the Coronet at all. No, she was going to meet an entirely different boyfriend at the Fischer Hotel in the Village. Gave the room number and every—"

"You believed that of me, Hal?" Dian had been quietly watching them lead her husband out.

"Hell, if you'll sneak off to meet Washburn, there's no telling what—"

"Got that note, Arneson?" Lieutenant Lewin held out his hand.

"Naw, I tossed it in a trash can down on Bleecker Street."

"Did you send it, Washburn?"

"No, damn it," denied the young actor. "This guy is full of baloney. He and his boss were always imagining that Nancy was up to some—"

"Who might Nancy be?" asked the lieutenant.

"He means me," explained Dian. "My real name's Nancy Washburn."

"To some people it looked overprotective," said Arneson, frowning. "But this is show business and we were only protecting a valuable property."

I asked him, "How'd you know Manheim'd been killed?"

He glared at me. "Who asked you to butt in again? Didn't we make it clear on that train that we didn't want any help from you or Groucho?"

"It's commencing to appear," said Groucho, "that you would have been wise to let us lend a hand on the Super Chief after somebody tried to shuffle Manheim off."

"That was our problem," the big man told him. "We didn't need a baggy-pants clown to interfere."

"My pants may be roomy," admitted Groucho, "but they are, sir, far from baggy. In fact, my pants have been held up as examples of natty dressing. James Fenimore Cooper it was who held them up as examples of Natty Bumppo. But he was full of cute tricks like that and back at the stockade we paid him no never mind."

128

"I'd like to know more about this attempt on Manheim's life that took place on the train," said Lieutenant Lewin.

"You can breathlessly await the full and lurid account that will appear in next month's issue of *True Confessions,*" Groucho said, "or I can drop in on you tomorrow and tell all."

"Tomorrow," said Lewin. "About ten."

"Why give a damn about that?" asked Arneson, jabbing a forefinger toward Washburn. "You've got the killer right there."

"What we've got," corrected the lieutenant, "is somebody we're going to talk to."

Shaking his head, Arneson took a few steps toward Dian. "C'mon, kid, I'll see you get back to the Waldorf."

She shook her head. "Groucho's going to escort me home."

"You've fallen a long way from grace," Groucho pointed out to the publicity man, "when a woman trusts *me* more than she does you, old boy."

About a half hour later Jane and I were walking, hand in hand, along Broadway. Groucho, after borrowing cab fare from me, had left to escort Dian Bowers back to her hotel. The marquee in front of a small news-reel theater we were passing asked, "War Near?"

"Hitler's going to move on Poland any day now," I said, glum.

"Think about the murder," advised my wife. "It'll take your mind off the world situation."

"I'm not feeling much like a detective at the moment," I admitted. "You and I and Groucho poked around backstage, questioned people, and almost stepped on several cops." I paused, shrugging. "We sure didn't find out a hell of a lot."

"We found out that nobody saw who propped Manheim's body up to fall out on the stage," she reminded. "It was dark backstage, with only an occasional flash of lightning and a lot of noise from the imitation thunder. Distracting—and somebody also knocked that stagehand out."

"Yeah, and all he remembers is that just before he got conked on the head he smelled some kind of leathery aftershave lotion."

"Could be a clue."

"Sure, we can ask Lewin to round up all the guys in Manhattan who smell like an old saddle."

Jane said, "Manheim was a pretty hefty guy. You'd have to be husky to lug him around backstage."

"Then the killer is probably a circus strong man who smells like an old saddle."

She let go of my hand, made a fist, and gave me a light poke in the upper arm. "C'mon, let's have a little less gloom," she suggested. "You and Groucho are eventually going to solve this."

"So you and Groucho seem to think. Myself, I—"

"Frank! Frank Denby! Hey, wait up."

I halted, glancing back over my shoulder. A small man, not more than twenty-five or so, was running along the night street in our wake. He had wavy dark hair and was dressed in the kind of expensive double-breasted suit you usually see in men's fashion magazines and not in real life.

Panting, he reached us. "Gee, I had to run a whole block to catch up with you, Frank," he said, smiling, holding out his hand. "Good to see you again."

I shook hands, not sure who he was. "Same here, I guess. Who exactly—"

"It's me. Nigel Windhurst," he announced.

That didn't mean anything to me.

Jane said, "You wrote *Make Mine Murder.*"

"Bingo," he said, grinning at her. "You're Frank's wife, huh? You ought to do something about his clothes."

"I've thought about burning them, but he gets cranky when I suggest that," she said, smiling sweetly. "Where does Frank know you from, Mr. Windhurst?"

"When Frank and I were buddies, my name was Stanley Sherman," he told her. "Many's the happy day we—"

"Stan?" I said, taking another look at him. "Where'd you get the dark wavy hair?"

"It's not entirely mine, Frank," he admitted. "You remember how they used to razz me on the *Los Angeles Times* because I was going prematurely bald? Well, when I struck it rich, I figured I could afford not to be prematurely bald anymore. I also capped my teeth."

I turned to Jane. "Stan was a copyboy on the *Times* when I—"

"Cub reporter," he corrected. "I came to Manhattan about four years ago and after the customary period of struggle, I clicked on Broadway. First with *The House on Gallows Hill,* which ran for fourteen months, and then with *Murder Gets Married.* That's still playing over at the Belasco. Sort of in the *Thin Man* vein, only a lot funnier and with a better plot." He sighed. "Gosh, when I heard you'd been backstage at *Make Mine Murder,* I got really excited, Frank." He grinned at Jane. "I haven't seen this mug for years, Mrs. Denby."

"Don't be so formal. You can call me Mrs. Mug."

The playwright chuckled. "Terrible about Daniel Manheim getting killed in the middle of our play," he said, taking on a more serious expression. "But, gee, that publicity's going to be great. 'Real Murder Halts *Make Mine Murder.*' A terrific headline, don't you think?"

"What'll you do," asked Jane, "if they arrest your leading man for the murder?"

Stan frowned. "That would be a bum break," he acknowledged. "But we could run with his understudy if we had to. Although, heck, I'd hate to see Bill Washburn get in any big trouble. He's such a nice guy."

"I didn't notice you backstage, Stan," I mentioned. "Were you—"

"Cops wouldn't let me back until they were finished nosing around. Gee, I told them I was the author, but that didn't mean much to them," he said. "I'd been watching the play from the back of the house when Manheim fell out of the closet."

We started walking along Broadway again and the erstwhile copy-boy fell in at my side. "So you didn't see anything that went on behind the scenes?" I asked.

"Not a darn thing, no," he answered. "Are you and Groucho Marx investigating this murder?"

"In our amateur capacity," I said.

"That's swell," said Stan. "You know what I think? Your escapades as crime busters would make for a terrific play. World-famous comedian joins forces with struggling writer. It'd be a sure hit."

Jane said, "But you'll let Frank struggle with the idea first, won't you? Before you turn it into a hit yourself."

He chuckled. "Hey, gosh, I've got enough great ideas of my own to last me for years, Mrs. Denby," he assured her. "Though if I did write a play about your husband and Groucho, I know who I could get to play your part."

"Besides me myself, you mean?"

"Willa Jerome," he announced with a pleased grin. "It turns out she's a great admirer of mine. Do you know who she is? Very talented British actress who's in a film called *Trafalgar—*"

"We've met," said Jane. "Mostly on trains."

I inquired, "How do you know she's a fan of yours, Stan? Was she at the opening tonight or—"

"Willa knew the Estlin Brothers in England, before they came over here to produce plays on Broadway," he explained. "She visited them last night, saw our final dress rehearsal, and took the time to tell me how terrific she thought *Make Mine Murder* was. She'd love, she mentioned, to do a really good stage play when she has some free time from the Hollywood grind."

"I was thinking," I said, "that Greta Garbo would be a better choice to portray my wife."

After watching my face for a few seconds, Stan chuckled again. "I see your husband's still the great kidder he was when we were reporters together in the old days, Mrs. Denby."

"Yes, he brings an enormous amount of laughter into my life," she admitted.

We reached a corner and the young playwright said, "I've got to go meet some people over at the Stork Club, so we'll say so long here."

"So long," I said.

"Listen, Frank, I think you and your wife owe it to yourselves to see the whole play some night soon," he said, holding out his hand. "Give me a ring—I'm in the book—Nigel Windhurst, remember—and I'll have them leave a pair of tickets for you at the box office. Sure nice meeting you, Mrs. Denby. Good night now." He went hurrying away into the bright-lit Broadway night.

"Dorothy Lamour," said Jane.

"Hm?"

"That's who I'd like to see play me on stage and screen."

"She doesn't look anything like you," I pointed out.

"Well, okay, you can cast somebody else, but she has to wear a sarong."

"It's interesting," I said.

"What?"

"The way Willa Jerome keeps recurring in our lives," I said.

Twenty-one

Two uniformed cops asked Groucho for his autograph before he reached Lieutenant Lewin's office in the precinct house. The lieutenant, wearing a different wrinkled suit, was sitting behind a slightly lopsided desk. The only thing in the office that wasn't faded was a small New York World's Fair poster tacked to the wall above one of the dented green filing cabinets.

Settling into the dark wooden chair facing the desk, Groucho inquired, "Who's your decorator? The reason I ask is, I'm planning on opening a nationwide chain of latrines and I just feel he'd be absolutely perfect for the job of furnishing them."

"How've you been, Groucho?"

"Well, Herb, about five months ago I thought I had an ingrown toenail, but that turned out to be a false alarm and I've been fit as a fiddle ever since. Are you going to hold Bill Washburn for murder?"

"We're going to be asking him a few more questions."

"He didn't do it."

"Maybe not," said the policeman.

"If Washburn had murdered Manheim, he wouldn't have been so stupid about it," Groucho pointed out. "He wouldn't have rigged the body to upstage him in his own play, and wouldn't have hidden the knife in his own dressing room."

Lewin nodded. 'There were no prints on the knife, in case you were wondering."

"I didn't expect you'd find Washburn's fingerprints on the thing."

When Lieutenant Lewin leaned back in his swivel chair, it made a rasping noise. "Now tell me about what happened while you show folks were traveling on the Super Chief from LA," he requested.

Groucho obliged, filling him in on the attempted assault on Manheim, and about both Arneson and me getting bopped on the head. In conclusion he said, "The means used by our mystery man on the train—blackjack and knife—are the same as those used by the person who actually killed Manheim, Herb."

"Similar, yes."

"Therefore, since Washburn was thousands of miles from the scene of the first crime, he isn't your man."

"Unless he heard about the attempt on Manheim—from his estranged wife, say—and thought it would be a nifty idea to imitate the style of that other assailant. Lots of copycats around, Groucho."

"He imitates the methods of somebody else, but then leaves the knife in his dressing room?"

"Some people think it's smart to act dumb."

"Here's something else to contemplate," put forth Groucho. "Both the late Manheim and his stooge Arneson worked mightily to put a lid on what happened. They didn't want any police called in, didn't want Frank Denby and me to investigate, didn't—"

"That last sounds sensible to me," cut in the policeman. "I don't think I'd want one of the Marx Brothers trying to find out who assaulted me."

"I'll ignore your cruel slur on my ratiocinative capabilities, Herbert," said Groucho magnanimously. "I merely suggest to you that Manheim acted like somebody who perhaps had something to hide. Mayhap he and Arneson didn't want to risk having the law look into their activities."

"Arneson told me only this morning, Groucho, that they were thinking only of the impending opening of *Saint Joan* and didn't want any negative publicity to detract from that. Guilty consciences had nothing to do with it."

"Malarkey," observed Groucho, locating a fresh cigar in the pocket of his umber-colored sports coat. "To a gent like Arneson there is no such thing as bad publicity, so long as you get your client's name in the news. If Manheim had been caught burning down an orphanage, Arneson would've sent out a press release headed *Producer of Saint Joan Has a Hot Time.*"

"You don't much like Arneson."

"I've never let him sign my dance card, no."

Lieutenant Lewin said, "Well, I won't stop you fellows from poking your noses into the Manheim case, Groucho. As I believe I've already mentioned, however, don't do a single damn thing that's going to put you in my way or screw up my investigation."

"We'll solve the mystery without your even noticing it, Herb," promised Groucho and lit his cigar.

The gold-trimmed revolving doors deposited me on the morning sidewalk in front of our hotel. Jane had preceded me and was waiting a few feet to the right of the gold-trimmed doorman.

"You're sure you want to go ahead with this?" she asked as I pulled up beside her.

"Didn't I once vow I'd follow you to the ends of the earth? And this sounds like a much shorter trip."

From the side pocket of her plaid coat she took a small notebook and flipped it open to a middle page. "Okay, most of the secondhand bookstores I want to visit are down around Fourth Avenue and vicinity," Jane said, consulting the list of addresses she'd copied out of the telephone directory. "If you think maybe you'll get bored while I hunt for old back issues of *Judge* and the *New Yorker* and the old *Life,* why then we can separate and meet for lunch someplace in Greenwich Village around one this—"

"No, I'm looking forward to browsing in a bunch of cluttered bookshops," I assured her. "After breathing all that clean pure air out in LA, I'm eager to inhale dust, mildew, bookworm droppings, and assorted effluvia."

"Since we're going to be spending most of the afternoon from three on with the people at the network," she said, slipping the little notebook away, "I just wanted to do something this morning that doesn't have a darn thing to do with *Hollywood Molly.* And collecting old cartoon magazines is the closest thing I have to a hobby."

I put my hand on her arm. "Hey, I'm willingly going with you," I reminded her. "Stop apologizing and rationalizing, okay?"

She nodded, smiling. "Manhattan does that to me," she confessed. "Brings out the schoolgirl. I get sort of giddy, excited, and insecure all at the same time. But . . . what is it, Frank?"

I was looking beyond her and the expression on my face had become what you might have called mixed. "Groucho is approaching from the direction of Sixth Avenue."

Jane glanced over her shoulder. "So he is, and he looks quite purposeful."

"For Groucho, yes."

Unlit cigar clenched in his teeth and pointing skyward, arms swinging at his sides, knees slightly bent, Groucho was making his way toward us through the midmorning scatter of pedestrians.

He was still about five feet away from us when a plump woman stepped into his path.

"Why, it's Groucho Marx!" she exclaimed, very pleased.

"It is? And here I thought it was probably Bastille Day."

The woman asked him, "What's the name of your next movie?"

"Well, if it's a boy, we're going to call it *Cimarron,*" he answered. "And if it's a girl, *Lupe Velez.*"

She giggled. "Mr. Marx, you're spoofing me."

"Oh, no, I'd never do that in a public place, my dear woman," he said. "However, I'd be perfectly happy spoofing you in the privacy of my hotel room. If you drop up there of an evening, we'll spoof till the cows come home. Although I'm somewhat doubtful that the whole herd can fit into that dinky elevator. But then that's not my problem, let Neville Chamberlain worry about it. That's why we elected him president, after all."

"Chamberlain isn't president, he's—"

"Well, see? I haven't read a newspaper for over a week and I'm completely out of touch." Bending some, he caught her hand, kissed it, and eased around her. "And now, good-bye."

"Good morning, Groucho," said Jane. "You're looking very dapper."

He frowned down at himself. "I am? I'll have to complain to my valet about that," he said. "But let's get to the point of this meeting. Rollo, there are some matters about the case I want to discuss with you. Are you free?"

"As a matter of fact, Jane and I—"

"Frank, stay with Groucho," cut in Jane. "I don't mind roaming the bookstores by myself."

"You're sure?"

"Pretty near absolutely." She leaned toward me and kissed me on the cheek. "I'll see you back here at the Saint Norbert around two."

Groucho observed, "You're an exceptional woman."

"I am," she agreed and asked the doorman to get her a taxi.

Groucho and I found an unoccupied bench and sat down.

He said, "Central Park is a mite roomier than Griffith Park. And there's a better class of squirrels."

"What happened to Bill Washburn?"

"That's one of the topics I wanted to talk about, Rollo," he answered. "The police are holding him for further questioning, but it doesn't look like they're going to charge him with anything."

"For now?"

"There's no guarantee that they won't eventually arrest him for murdering Manheim," said Groucho. "There are those, apparently, who'd like to do that right now, but Lieutenant Lewin isn't completely convinced that Washburn is a half-wit."

"Since only a half-wit would hide the murder weapon in his own dressing room."

"Exactly," he said, nodding. "Unless, of course, Washburn is trying to be tricky and using the only-a-half-wit gambit to try to outfox the law."

"That knife really is the one that was used on Manheim?"

"That it is. A fairly common type of kitchen knife that's sold all across this great land of ours."

"Any fingerprints on the thing?"

"Nary a one, no," said Groucho. "No footprints either, meaning our killer wore gloves *and* shoes."

"I suppose nobody saw anyone suspicious sneaking into Washburn's dressing room to plant the knife, huh?"

"If they did, they're maintaining a discreet silence." Groucho leaned back on the green bench. "One of the problems we face, and a major reason for sticking with this case and finding the real killer, is that Bill Washburn makes a dandy candidate for the role of killer."

"Yeah, I know."

"Manheim stole his wife, persuaded her to separate from him, changed her name, and tried to prevent them from ever seeing each other again," amplified Groucho. "Those are some pretty good reasons for not being fond of Manheim."

"Then last night Manheim shows up in person to threaten Washburn," I picked up. "They have a noisy argument, yell at each other, and—"

"Whenever I have noisy arguments, I try never to speak above a whisper," said Groucho. "I also refrain from slugging my opponents during a debate or leaving them sprawled in my dressing room afterwards."

"You have to admit that Washburn had motive and opportunity," I said. "Last night anyway."

"But he wasn't on the Super Chief when the earlier attempt was made on Manheim," said Groucho. "Which leads me to speculate that the true killer is one of our fellow passengers."

"It wasn't me or Jane and it wasn't you," I began. "And—"

"It couldn't have been me," said Groucho, "because I always refuse to take part in any mystery case where the killer turns out to be the private detective."

"The fact that Dian Bowers was with you at the time of the murder rules her out, too."

"Yes, by risking her reputation by being seen in public with me, the child provided herself with an ironclad alibi."

I paused to watch three guys in business suits ride by on bicycles. "I'm wondering about Arneson."

Groucho was leaning toward a grey squirrel who was approaching us across the slanting Central Park stretch of grass. "I know what you're going to say," he told the squirrel. "Harpo's your favorite." He returned his attention to me. "Arneson was supposed to be dedicated to protecting Manheim."

"Sure, but when he got to the theater last night, he wanted everybody to know he was just showing up for the first time."

Groucho took a book of paper matches out of the pocket of his rust-colored sports coat, lit his unlit cigar. "We might jot Arneson down on our tentative list of suspects," he said finally, exhaling a swirl of smoke. "But I'm dubious—and, please, no Smith and Dale routines."

"That dancer—Len Cowan. The guy who hates Manheim for ruining his sister," I said. "He's a possibility, too."

"Yep, we'd best find out why he isn't dancing his heart out in Chicago as originally planned."

"I'll check with May Sankowitz—she seems to be a chum of his."

After taking a long thoughtful puff on his cigar, Groucho said, "And we ought to find out more about the activities of Willa Jerome and her coterie."

"I forgot to tell you that she was at the theater on Monday night."

"Oh, so? A whole night early for the opening?"

"She's a friend of the producers and attended the final dress rehearsal." I told him about our running into Stanley Sherman, alias Nigel Windhurst.

"You're falling behind on your acorn quota," Groucho told the squirrel, who was standing on his hind legs and eyeing us from a couple feet away. "I've been thinking, Frank—which is something I try to do at least once every day, rain or shine. I've been thinking that it's somewhat odd that two of the women who are involved in this mess were also chummy with the late Nick Sanantonio."

"Meaning there might be some kind of link between the gambler's murder and Manheim's?"

He shrugged his left shoulder and took another puff of his cigar. "Might be a connection, might just be a coincidence," he said. "Or mayhap one of the damsels is a jinx and every guy she comes near gets bumped off."

"I'll contact one of my informants back in Los Angeles, dig up some more about Sanantonio's relationship with these two actresses," I offered. "You should be able to get Dian Bowers to provide you with some details of what really went on between her and Sanantonio and if Manheim ties in somehow."

"I'm going to see the lady in question right after my *Mikado* rehearsal this afternoon," he said. "I'll ask a few deft and subtle questions, not to mention a whole batch of blunt and offensive ones."

"Manheim had a reputation for being extremely protective of his protégées," I said. "If Sanantonio was tomcatting around Dian, maybe Manheim warned him off and that annoyed some of the guys in the Mob."

"It's not a good idea to annoy the Mob, no," he said, stretching up off the bench. "All this pastoral tranquility is giving me palpitations. Let's move on."

We moved on and the squirrel went bouncing away toward the nearest tree.

Twenty-two

The Maximus Publications Building rose a dozen-and-a-half stories above Lexington Avenue in the East 50s. The eleventh floor was devoted to movie magazines, pulp fiction magazines, and comic books.

As I made my way back to May Sankowitz's temporary office, I noticed cover proofs for *Movietown, Hollywood Screen, Snappy Detective, Snappy Western, Hyperman,* and *Capt. Starr Comics* scattered on desks, pinned to drawing boards, tacked to corkboard walls. There were about thirty people scattered around at desks, boards, and in cubbyhole offices. About half of them were talking either to each other or on telephones and just about all of them were smoking. It was pretty much like a newsroom, though not as noisy.

A thin young cartoonist held up a rough sketch of a comic book cover when I passed through his section of the big room. "I need an outside opinion, pal. What do you think?"

The work was untitled. "Is that Hyperman?"

"Naw, it's Capt. Starr."

I noticed that the hero did have a star emblazoned on his broad, sketchy chest. He was wrestling with a gorilla who wore a Nazi armband, intent on saving a blonde girl who was about to be bronzed in a huge smoking cauldron.

I said, "It's action-packed."

"I know, but is it believable?"

"Matter of fact, I just witnessed a similar scene at the corner of Madison and Fifty-third," I assured him.

"Another wiseass." Slapping the drawing back against his slanted drawing board, he turned his back on me.

Finding a door marked *Hollywood Screen,* I tapped on it.

"If you're not Frank Denby," called May Sankowitz, "you can go to hell."

"What a break for me that I'm the world's only existing Frank Denby," I said, entering the small, narrow office.

May was seated behind the cluttered desk, legs up, shoes off. Her hair was now a quiet shade of red. "Throw that crap on the floor, Frank dear, and sit yourself down."

"New shade of hair," I mentioned as I removed the stack of *Hollywood Screen* page proofs and some photos off the only other chair in the little office. The top photos were glossies of Dian Bowers. She looked very demure.

"Yeah, this is my Manhattan hair color," explained my writer friend. "It's not as subtle as my LA hue."

"True." I settled into the chair.

"The closer you get to fifty, the more obvious you tend to be." May swung her legs off the desktop, sat up straight. "Before I provide you any more free and valuable inside info, dear, tell me every blessed thing you know about the Manheim murder."

"I got there after he was killed, also after he fell out of the closet and onto the stage at the Coronet," I told May. "Most of what I know is hearsay."

"Firsthand hearsay is just fine." She made an impatient start-talking gesture with her right hand. "Tell me."

I gave her a quick account of what I knew. "Now, as to why I—"

"And they arrested Bill Washburn?"

"Not exactly, May. They seem to be holding him for questioning."

"My deal to accompany the so-called Dian Bowers as she gets introduced to New York City has been postponed," she said. "But now I think I can work up something a lot juicier. *I Stood By My Killer Husband!* Perfect for our moronic subscribers."

"You can run a picture of Washburn wrestling a gorilla on the cover."

"Huh?"

I shook my head. "Nothing. I've been reading too much Capt. Starr," I said. "I want to know about your friend Len Cowan."

"Who?"

"The dancer, the guy who was supposed to be part of the Chicago *Step Right Up* company," I said. "I saw him with you when we arrived in New York the other morning."

"Leonard, sure. Cute kid, though a little young for me. And a lousy temper."

"Why isn't he in Chicago?"

"Oh, he got a better offer and quit."

"What kind of offer?"

"Something to do with a musical show that's going to be staged at the World's Fair. Supposed to pay better and Leonard's going to be a featured dancer in it."

"Know the name of the show?"

May rested both elbows on the desk. "Why all this interest in an erstwhile chorus boy, dear?"

"He may tie in with the Manheim business somehow. Groucho and I are interested in—"

"I thought you swore to me that you fellas had quit playing detective."

"That was before Manheim got killed. Now, to make sure that Washburn doesn't get railroaded for the crime, we—"

"Why do you give a good god damn about what happens to a one-time B-movie actor?"

"We're also concerned about Dian Bowers."

"Ah, yes, right. Just like the Lone Ranger and Tonto, you're dedicated to looking after sweet innocent maidens."

"It's a little more complex than—"

"Only hitch, sweet, is that little Dian doesn't quite qualify for the role of dewy-eyed virgin."

"Yeah, I figured that after marrying Washburn, she lost her status as—"

"I was alluding to the fact that she's also spent some time in the sack with Nick Sanantonio," said May. "That sort of thing can—"

"Is this Hollywood gossip or do you know for—"

"Most gossip, Frank, is built on a firm foundation of truth," May reminded me. "And I know for a fact that the now-saintly Dian was as cozy as you can get with that gangster."

"What ended it?"

"Don't know, but I'd guess that Manheim pulled in her reins."

"I hear he did things like that."

"He kept a very close watch on his discoveries." She glanced at her wristwatch. "And now, dear, I have to attend a press conference and two screenings simultaneously. Bye."

"Good-bye," I said and left.

Groucho, as he later told me, stepped from the afternoon brightness of the Manhattan sidewalk into the shadowy quiet of a tearoom. The name of the place was the Queen of Cups and it was on a side street at the edge of the Gramercy Park area.

Even though there were only a few patrons in the small tea parlor, he didn't initially notice Dian Bowers among them. At the table nearest the tiny foyer a large blonde woman in a vaguely Gypsy outfit was using a deck of oversized tarot cards to give a reading to an uneasy tourist couple.

"Over here," said a quiet voice off in the shadows on his right.

Dian was sitting alone at a small circular table. She wore a simple grey suit and dark glasses, no makeup, and a scarf over her close-cropped hair.

"What news?" asked Groucho, sitting opposite the actress.

She gave a small sigh. "They're still holding Bill, but the attorney I hired for him tells me they'll be releasing him in time for tonight's performance of *Make Mine Murder.*"

"You seem far from pleased by the news."

"I think maybe they're only giving him enough rope to hang himself."

"He's innocent, so he can't very well do that," he pointed out. "And we intend to find out who the real killer is." He paused, watching her. "You do believe Bill's innocent, don't you?"

After a few silent seconds, she answered, "I do, yes, but . . ."

"But?"

"It's only that . . ." She shook her head, leaned closer to him, lowered her voice. "There are some things that the police don't know about yet."

"Such as?"

"Well, out in Los Angeles last year—"

"Would the gentleman like a cup of tea?" inquired the thin waitress who appeared beside their table. She, too, was in a vaguely Gypsy costume.

"Are you referring to me?" said Groucho, eyebrows rising. "If so, I must warn you that there are such things as slander laws in this state, miss, and calling me a gentleman in public constitutes—"

"Oh, you're Groucho Marx," the waitress suddenly realized. "That explains it. For a moment, you see, I thought you were just another rude middle-aged moron trying to be funny."

"Right on both counts," he said. "I'll have the same thing the lady's having." When the waitress departed, he frowned across at Dian. "You were about to reveal some deep dark secrets in your husband's past."

"I didn't behave too well to Bill," she said quietly. "I let Manheim persuade me that it would be a great idea to separate from my husband. I . . . well, I pretty much turned over my life to Manheim." She tapped her fingertip against the handle of her teacup. "At one point Bill got very angry and tried to get in to see me. Manheim had some men who were sort of extra bodyguards . . . or maybe bouncers is a better word. Anyway, I'm pretty certain that Manheim had them work Bill over. Beat him up, then warn him to keep away from me."

"Where were you residing at the time?"

She looked down at the crisp white tablecloth. "Well, okay. I did live at Manheim's mansion for a few months."

Groucho said, "Of course, I'm not the average husband, but I think I, too, might be a trifle upset if my wife was domiciled with a movie mogul."

"I didn't say it was a smart thing to do. But I did it."

"Being beaten up on orders from Manheim—that would give Bill one more reason for wanting to kill him," Groucho said. "It definitely adds an item to his list of motives for murdering the guy. Who knows about it?"

"Enough people," she answered, sipping her tea.

"Then eventually Lieutenant Lewin is going to get wind of it."

"I'm afraid that'll happen, yes."

Groucho's tea arrived. He ignored it and rested an elbow on the table. "There's another rumor that's come to my attention," he told her. "And I'd like a bit more information."

"Something else about Bill?"

"About you," he corrected.

She gave him a perplexed look. "I'll tell you anything I can, if it'll help my husband."

"You knew Nick Sanantonio a lot better than you let on when you were chatting about him on the train," he said.

"That's not true."

Groucho said, "So your story is you were just friends?"

"If you're supposed to be a friend of mine," she said, angry, "then I don't know what purpose it serves to dig up some cheap gossip about me."

"I'm supposed to be a friend of both you and Bill," he corrected.

148

"Sanantonio was also killed and it occurs to me that there might be some connection between the two murders. If you maintain you barely knew him, then we'll drop it and I'll search around for—"

"All right, Groucho," the actress said. "I guess it won't do much good to pretend that I've been a loyal wife ever since Bill and I split up." She took a slow deep breath in, then slowly exhaled. "Yes, I had an affair with Nick. It lasted for a couple of months and it might be dragging on still if Manheim hadn't cracked down."

"Cracked down how?"

"He had Arneson contact some people and they contacted Nick," she answered, her voice faint. "Basically they told him to lay off me or he'd be in serious trouble."

"Sanantonio agreed?"

"For a while," she answered.

Groucho narrowed his left eye, studying her. "Meaning what exactly?"

"I think Nick broke up with whoever else it was he'd been seeing recently," she said. "He apparently decided he'd like to start dating me again. He telephoned me a few times, tried to come see me. I wasn't interested, though, and that ended it."

"Did it now?" Groucho picked up his teacup, then set it down. "Were Manheim, Arneson, and their assorted heavies aware of this newest attempt by Sanantonio?"

She shook her head. "I don't believe so," she answered, not too confidently. "But then there wasn't much about my life and times that they didn't know."

"Is Willa Jerome a pal of yours?"

"Hardly," she replied. "She was on the Super Chief with us and we exchanged hellos. That's about it. Why?"

"She was, supposedly, another one of Sanantonio's girlfriends."

"I've heard gossip that she was, but he never mentioned her to me," said Dian. "I hear she's not that terrific an actress and that she made all kinds of trouble during the shooting of *Trafalgar Square.*"

"Everybody in the movie business isn't as easygoing and even-tempered as I am," he reminded. He tasted his tea, winced.

"Listening to myself talk just now," she said after a moment, "I don't sound especially saintly."

"*Saint Joan* was a movie," he told her. "And this is real life or at least a reasonable facsimile."

Twenty-three

From the large windows of Conference Room 3 on the eleventh floor of the Amalgamated Radio Network building on Madison Avenue you could look out at the surrounding office buildings and a patch of clear blue afternoon sky. I was doing that when the Vice President In Charge Of Night Time Programming came striding into the room.

He was followed by a trim brunette in a tan suit who announced, "Mr. Gramatky apologizes for being ten minutes late."

"He's twenty minutes late," I said to Jane, who was standing beside me at the big window.

"He's probably operating on Eastern Executive Time," she suggested, leading me back to the oval conference table.

Wardell Gramatky was a plump, well-groomed man in his early forties, resembling a sort of preshrunk Paul Whiteman. "Very happy to meet you, Miss Danner," he said, installing himself at the end of the table. "And your gifted husband."

As soon as he sat, his secretary came around to our side of the cherry-wood table to give us each a fresh yellow legal tablet and a brand-new mechanical pencil. "To keep track of what's going on," she explained.

The only other person at the meeting was Milt Banion, the lean blonde executive from the McKay and Forman advertising agency. He was in charge of producing the *Hollywood Molly* radio show for the network.

"Does the afternoon find you well, Milt?" inquired Gramatky.

"Never better, Wardell. And you?"

"My ruptured disc is acting up and I'm afraid I'll be heading straight from our little meeting to my chiropractor." He smiled briefly. "But let's get down to business. Jane—if I may call you that?—Jane, I've read all the proposed story lines for the *Hollywood Molly* programs and I love them. Miss Farmer will testify that I chuckled more than once while reading the batch."

"He did," confirmed the dark-haired secretary.

Jane said, "That's very gratifying." She began to doodle on her tablet.

"There's really only one story idea we can't use on ARN and that's because—which you had no way of knowing—it doesn't conform to our standards," said Gramatky, a little sadly. "While murder is perfectly permissible on our successful mystery shows—such as *The Casebook of Dr. Thorndyke, The Amazing Mr. Woo,* and *Bentley of Scotland Yard*— we simply frown at using murder on a comedy show."

"It goes beyond frowning," said Banion. "You absolutely can't have any killings on a comedy show."

Jane squeezed my hand below the level of the table. "I'm certainly glad you've cleared that up for us, Mr. Gramatky," she said sweetly. "As you know, Frank wrote Groucho Marx's comedy mystery show for two seasons and there—"

"Different networks, different standards." Gramatky smoothed at his thin moustache.

I asked, "Are we allowed a jewel theft or a burglary now and then?"

Gramatky considered. "If you absolutely must, but we'd like to see that sort of thing only rarely."

Banion suggested, "This would be a good time to bring up the dog."

"What dog?" asked Jane and I, just about simultaneously.

"Do you have that memo from Research?" Gamatky asked his secretary.

From one of the three manila folders before her, Miss Farmer extracted a mimeographed sheet. "Here it is."

Gramatky took the page, scanned it. "Yes, we've found that most people like dogs better than cats," he told us.

"And?" asked Jane.

Banion said, "We'll be changing Molly's cat—Boswell, is it?—to a dog. Young boys relate to dogs better, so does the average family. And I can get one of the top dog impersonators in the business to play the—"

"Boswell is a cat," said Jane. She pressed so hard with her mechanical pencil that the lead snapped.

"In your comic strip, yes," agreed Gramatky. "For the purposes of our radio show, however, we—"

"He's going to remain a cat," Jane said firmly. "If you guys want a dog, we'll come up with a new name."

"Dorgan," I offered.

"We'll call him Dorgan, sure," said Jane, nodding.

"If Research determines that the name is acceptable," said Gramatky, touching his moustache again.

"It doesn't have to be Molly's dog," said Banion. "It can just as well be her brother's."

"She doesn't have a brother," I reminded.

"It's our feeling over at McKay and Forman, as I've mentioned before, Miss Danner, that a kid brother will add a heck of a lot of appeal to the show."

"Hooey," remarked Jane.

"Let's get back to that dog for a moment, Milt," said Gramatky. "It occurs to me that a dog will sit very well with old Dr. Weber."

"Right. He loves dogs."

"Who," asked Jane, "in the heck is Dr. Weber?"

Banion replied, "He's very interested in sponsoring the *Hollywood Molly* show."

"We're pretty certain," added Gramatky, "that he'll sign up for a trial thirteen weeks."

Leaning toward Jane, Miss Farmer said, "Dr. Weber's Tooth Powder—Regular and Mint Flavor."

" 'For That Million Dollar Smile,' " added Banion, smiling.

Jane said, "We'll concede on a dog. But no kid brother for Molly."

Gramatky nodded and scribbled something on his own yellow pad. "What sort of dog do you have in mind?"

The meeting went on for another hour and ten minutes.

Twilight was settling on Manhattan and Groucho, softly whistling "I've Got a Little List" from *The Mikado,* was slouching his way up Broadway.

When he halted at the curb for a traffic signal, a plump woman pedestrian in a tan cloth coat came to a stop beside him. She glanced casually over at him, then gave a surprised gasp. She said, "You look like Groucho Marx."

"And that's precisely why I'm suing my plastic surgeon," he replied. "I was supposed to end up looking like Cesar Romero."

"But you *are* Groucho Marx, aren't you?"

"Certainly, but that's no reason why I have to look like him."

The light changed and he went loping away across the street.

Halfway up on the next block Groucho entered Alfie's Pub.

Leo Haskell, the *New York Daily Tab* columnist, was sitting at the first booth to the left of the doorway. A pudgy bald man in a wrinkled sharkskin suit was leaning over the table, trying to show him some publicity photos.

"She's a real looker, Leo."

"Average puss, average stems."

"She's always coming up with witty lines."

"So you claim, buster."

"She's about to take over the lead in *Kick Up Your Heels.*"

"It's a long shot."

"One damn mention in your column, Leo." The perspiring bald man

154

held his thumb and forefinger less than an inch apart. "Just this much space. It would be a terrific break for the kid."

"You can shuffle off now, Otto," suggested Haskell, noticing Groucho's approach. "Park your cadaver, Julius."

"Glad to see you again, Groucho," said the plump man as Groucho seated himself across from the columnist. "You remember me, don't you?"

"I would, except that not ten minutes ago I was stricken with severe amnesia."

"I'm Otto Zimmer, the publicity guy."

"You know, I was guessing you were Otto Zimmer the Gypsy violinist," said Groucho. "Which shows how amnesia can play hob with your memory."

"Take a powder, Otto," advised Haskell, pointing a thumb in the direction of the door to the dim-lit bar.

"See you guys around." The rumpled Zimmer, sliding the photos back into his scuffed briefcase, made his way out of the moderately crowded room.

Haskell picked up his glass of Chivas Regal scotch and took a sip. "So you're going to be appearing at the World's Fair this Friday, my boy?"

"We'll be putting on an informal rehearsal of *The Mikado* at the Bascom Music Pavilion out there, yes," replied Groucho. "It's a one-shot charity festivity that our producer and Grover Whalen cooked up. They only got around to mentioning it to me this afternoon. I was planning to enter a six-day bike race on Friday, but now I'll have to wait around until they hold a five-day bike race."

Haskell made the dry barking noise that he used for a laugh. "I see old age hasn't dimmed your sense of humor, Julius," he said, taking another sip. "Can I buy you a drink?"

"I'd rather you buy me a controlling interest in the Brooklyn Dodgers, but I'll settle for a ginger ale."

The columnist signaled a waiter, then said, "I'm plugging your Friday clambake at the fair in my column mañana, Julius. You'll have standing room only, pal."

"That's too bad. I was hoping I'd get to sit down."

"You never get tired of kidding around."

"As a matter of fact, Leo, I do. I'm seriously considering quitting show business and taking up folk painting. I plan to call myself Grandma Marx."

Somebody dropped a nickel in the jukebox and it commenced playing "The Beer Barrel Polka."

After the waiter took Groucho's order and moved away, Haskell said, "Are you and your brothers really going to make more movies?"

"We're committed to doing two more for MGM."

Haskell shook his head. "I was going to suggest you bail out while you're ahead, but from what I hear about *At the Circus,* it's already too late for that."

"What we're going for now is an item in Ripley," explained Groucho. "First comedy team to make a motion picture without one single laugh in it. We're getting closer every film." He hunched his shoulders slightly and rested his elbows on the table. "One of the reasons I wanted to chat with you, Leo, is because you know a lot of scuttlebutt and—"

"You really are working on this Manheim thing, huh?" said Haskell. "You're trying to prove Bill Washburn isn't the guy who did it."

"I'm interested in the case," admitted Groucho. "Have you heard anything about who else might want to—"

"You and that writer pal of yours had some luck solving mysteries out on the Coast," said the columnist. "You even outwitted Sherlock Holmes."

"We outwitted a hambone actor who was playing Sherlock on the silver screen," corrected Groucho. "Have you—"

"If you solve this one, Julius, will you give me an exclusive? *Clown Catches Killer!* That's front-page stuff, pal."

"Not to mention alliterative." Groucho glanced at his just-arrived glass of ginger ale. "Who else might want to do Manheim in?"

"There are a lot of contenders," answered Haskell. "Of course, I'd put Washburn high on the list. Manheim gave Washburn's missus the usual treatment. Seduces her away from her marriage, tries to turn her into a movie star, and, for good measure, has her hubby worked over to keep him in line."

"You know for a fact he did that to Washburn—had him beaten up?"

"You've got to follow my damn column more often—I'm in twenty-six papers out in California," Haskell said. "I had an item about that last year. 'What low-budget fillum thesper got a darkalley drubbing at the behest of what Tinselvania moompitcher nabob?' "

"Give me a rough translation."

"Manheim hired some heavies to work the Washburn lad over," replied the columnist. "My sources out in Movietown tell me that Manheim made a habit of discouraging his rivals in that fashion, Julius." He frowned in the direction of the jukebox across the smoky room. "I loathe that goddamn song."

"You wouldn't have a list of the folks who benefited from beatings that Manheim arranged?"

"Nope," said Haskell, shaking his head. "Do you figure one of his victims decided to get even by writing the poor sap into *Make Mine Murder*?"

"Well, revenge does make a dandy motive."

"Suppose Manheim had been involved in something more serious than having somebody worked over?"

Groucho sat up, eyebrows rising. "Such as what—a murder?"

"This is only a very vague rumor so far," answered Haskell. "Much too vague even for my column."

"And who, according to your vague sources, was the recipient of Manheim's attentions?"

"Soon as I have specifics that I can hint at," promised the columnist, "you'll be among the first to know, pal." He stood up. "I've got to catch a nap before I commence my nightly round of hot spots, my boy. Keep in touch, huh?"

"Oh, I will," promised Groucho.

After six rings, somebody answered the phone at the Ivy Hotel out in Los Angeles. "Hold on," requested a blurred voice.

I held on and in about two minutes a different voice inquired, "Yeah?"

"Tim O'Hearn's room, please."

"Don't think he's in."

"Try him," I advised whoever was manning the switchboard at the second-rate downtown hotel where my informant was living.

"Okay, buddy, hold on."

Some buzzing and crackling followed. Then O'Hearn said, "Yeah, hello?"

"It's Frank."

"Which Frank?"

"Frank Denby, Tim, the same guy who phoned you a couple hours ago."

O'Hearn coughed. "Jesus, Frank, I got a real lousy cold."

"You told me. Have you found out anything?"

He coughed again—a dry, rattling cough. "How much money did you say you were going to wire me?"

"Ten bucks."

"That's what got here, Frank, but I thought you promised me twenty."

"Ten in front."

"This isn't, you know, as simple as you made it sound," complained my longtime informant. "Not only is it a damn tough assignment, Frank, but it could be dangerous. I'm going to have to have at least twenty more."

"Okay, but tell me what you've dug up so far."

He coughed some more. "This cough syrup I'm taking doesn't work at all," he said.

"What sort of word is floating around out there about Nick Sanantonio's murder?" I reminded.

"The cops don't have this yet," said O'Hearn, "but I hear that one of the guys who was in on the killing is no longer among the living."

"Who was he?"

"Don't have a name yet, but he was an import."

I asked, "Who imported him?"

O'Hearn coughed yet again. "Way I hear it this movie guy who got bumped off back there where you are, Frank, maybe had a hand in hiring some guys to do the job."

"You mean Daniel Manheim?"

"That's him, yeah."

"The idea being that Manheim got hold of some freelance hoods to kill off Sanantonio," I said, frowning. "Why?"

"Not sure yet."

"Does it have something to do with Dian Bowers?"

"I haven't been able to find that out so far, Frank," O'Hearn told me. "When I'm, you know, working for chickenfeed, it takes longer to—"

"What about Willa Jerome?"

"Yeah, she had a hot-and-heavy fling with Sanantonio all right. Word is, he called it quits and she ended up carrying the torch."

I asked him, "And who took care of the hired killer—Salermo?"

"Pretty sure it was some of his boys, although nobody'll ever prove that." He began coughing again.

"Okay. Keep digging on this, Tim."

"Huh? I didn't hear you because I was hacking away."

"Get me as much more information as you can. I'll call you again either tonight or early tomorrow."

"Wire me the rest of the dough," he said and hung up.

Twenty-four

The next afternoon, as soon as the *Mikado* rehearsal was over, several reporters descended on Groucho.

"Is this about what people will get when they attend the rehearsal at the World's Fair tomorrow afternoon?" asked the guy from the *New York Post*.

"Pretty much so, except I'll be singing on key." Groucho settled into a folding chair along one wall of the practice hall.

"Have you been out to the fairgrounds yet?" asked the *Daily News* reporter.

"Not since long before the fair. I used to hang around there quite a bit years ago when it was a garbage dump, though."

"Are you looking forward to visiting the World's Fair?" asked the *Daily Mirror*.

"Yes, and I think it'll be even more fun than the garbage dump."

The man from the *World-Telegram* said, "Word is that *At the Circus* is funnier than *Room Service*."

Groucho frowned. "That's not saying much. *The Lower Depths* is funnier than *Room Service*."

"Is it true," asked the *New York Times,* "that you're planning to quit the movies?"

"Yes, ever since I was passed over for the lead in *Gone with the Wind,* I decided to retire from the screen," he answered. "And I think I would've made a delightful Scarlett O'Hara."

The reporter from the *News* asked him, "What about the murder of Daniel Manheim?"

"I didn't do it."

"Are you investigating the case?"

"Investigating isn't exactly the word I'd apply," answered Groucho. "Mucking up is the apt phrase."

The *Times* said, "Aren't you being overly modest, Groucho? You solved several murder cases out in California."

"Sure, but that's California, where murderers aren't as smart as they are here in the big city," he pointed out. "And the light's better."

The reporter from the *Sun* asked, "About Manheim, Groucho—can you tell us who done it?"

Groucho extracted a cigar from a pocket of his navy blue blazer. "No, but I can tell you who *didn't* do it. And that's Bill Washburn."

"Anything else to pass along?"

Groucho stood. "Look me up in a couple more days, lads," he advised. "I'll tell you everything I know about the case."

"Why not tell us now?"

"That would spoil the suspense." Unwrapping the cigar, he headed for the doorway.

In the hallway the assistant director of the show came up to him. "Somebody called for you, claimed it was important," he said, handing Groucho a memo and pointing at a small office. "You can use the telephone in there."

Dr. Dowling's speech was only very slightly slurred. "I wasn't sure if you remembered me, Mr. Marx," he was saying on the phone.

Groucho, perched on the edge of the small dark wood desk, said, "You are, my dear doctor, the most unforgettable character I have ever met. In fact, I've been meaning to write a piece to that effect for the *Reader's Digest,* but it keeps slipping my mind. And how may I be of service to you? We just got in a new supply of lumberjack jackets and they're all in your size. With each one we throw in a free whistle *and* a sturdy oak tree. For five bucks extra we throw in Nelson Eddy and—"

"I saw in Leo Haskell's column today that you'll be appearing at the World's Fair tomorrow."

"Exactly. We're putting on an informal rehearsal of *The Mikado.*"

The doctor said, "Willa Jerome is going to be touring the fair tomorrow afternoon. A publicity jaunt to promote *Trafalgar Square.* I'll be, as usual, tagging along."

"Well, if you can tear yourself away," invited Groucho, "drop in on our little madrigal. We'll be holding forth at the Bascom Music Pavilion, wherever that is, commencing at two-thirty P.M."

"Yes, there's something . . ." His voice trailed off.

"How's that, old man?"

"Well, there's something that's been coming back to me," said the doctor quietly. "It's a somewhat fuzzy recollection of events on the Super Chief."

"This is connected with Daniel Manheim's murder?"

Dr. Dowling hesitated. "As I believe I told you, I'm somewhat hazy about the journey," he said. "But for the past couple days I've been feeling very uneasy and I'm trying to jog my memory. It's not exactly something I can go to the police with. However, since I know you're working on the case in an unofficial sort of way, I'd like to talk the matter over with you."

"If you've got fuzzy notions and vague thoughts, I'm your man, Doc," Groucho assured him. "Is there anything a bit more specific you can tell me right now?"

Dr. Dowling said, "I'm hoping I'll be in a better position to do that tomorrow, Mr. Marx. I'll see you at the World's Fair."

"Okay. I'll tell them at the door to let you come backstage," promised Groucho.

"That'll be just fine."

Hanging up the receiver, Groucho sat on the edge of the desk for nearly five minutes.

I straightened up and pulled back from the portable typewriter I'd rented the day before at the Gotham Typewriter Shop over on Sixth Avenue. "Done," I announced, noticing that the afternoon was starting to fade outside.

Jane, legs tucked under her, had been sitting in an armchair going through the newspapers. "Want to read it to me?"

Tugging the final page of the second draft of our first *Hollywood Molly* radio script out of the machine, I answered, "Nope, no, not at all. As I recall, it was Aristotle who first advised, 'Don't read anything you've just written to the missus, fellas.' And it's remained sound advice even to this day."

"Okay, I'll take it into the bedroom later and read it to myself."

"So long as I don't hear any groans or cursing."

Jane said, "But seriously, Frank, what do you think?"

"Seriously, I think it's terrific," I answered. "Especially considering that we had to accommodate the whims, taboos, and totally irrational obsessions of your syndicate, the advertising agency, the network, and our potential sponsor."

"I hope you have Molly brushing her teeth a lot," said Jane. "In case we do land Dr. Weber's Tooth Powder as the sponsor."

"That's one of the things I'm a mite uneasy about," I confessed. "I have her keeping the toothbrush in her mouth throughout the entire show and I'm not completely convinced that it won't interfere with the delivery of her wisecracks."

"Don't see why it should." She smiled at me, stretched, and then tapped the scatter of newspapers on her lap. "I see by the papers that Manheim Productions is going ahead with the premiere of *Saint Joan* next week."

"I bet a spokesman for the company said that Manheim would've wanted it that way."

"Arneson himself made just such an announcement," said Jane. "And they're turning the initial screening into a combination premiere and memorial service. Conrad Nagel is flying in from the coast to act as master of ceremonies."

"We can but hope, when our time comes, that we get such a send-off."

"You can have Conrad Nagel. Me, I'd prefer Louis Armstrong singing 'I'll Be Glad When You're Dead, You Rascal You.' "

Gathering up the twenty-six typed pages of script, I rose from the sofa. My bones produced several small, odd creakings. Shuffling the pages into a coherent and neat stack, I placed them on the coffee table beside the rented Royal portable. "Think I'll make one more try to get in touch with O'Hearn."

"You still haven't been able to contact the guy?"

"Not once today, no," I answered. "Every time I telephone his tumbledown hotel in LA, they say my informant hasn't come back yet. I hope he isn't—"

The phone rang.

Jane picked up the receiver from the end table next to her chair. "Hello," she said and listened for a moment. "Let me take a look. No, he's not down in the street rolling in the gutter. What's that? Hold on. No, I don't see him out in Central Park gamboling with underage convent girls. Oh, wait, Groucho, he just came in from attending the stevedores' picnic." She handed me the phone. "Groucho."

"So I deduced. Yes, sir?"

"Rollo, I am about to offer you a once—twice at best—in a lifetime opportunity," he began.

"We already have a set of the *Encyclopaedia Britannica.*"

"This will be even more enlightening. How'd you like to accompany me to the New York World's Fair tomorrow out at the aptly named Flushing Meadows?"

"You're putting on that charity rehearsal, aren't you?"

"I will be using my God-given angelic voice for the sake of charity, yes," he replied. "And I'm also scheduled to meet with Dr. Dowling, who is perhaps better known as the Pickled Physician of Pasadena."

"With Willa Jerome's personal doctor, huh?"

"He's implied he has something to tell us about the Manheim case."

"Such as?"

"No details at this time," said Groucho. "You can bring the wife in case you don't want to travel alone with a noted roué such as myself."

"What time?"

"My benevolent producer is sending a limousine at noon tomorrow to convey me to the fairgrounds. Originally he planned on providing a Good Humor wagon, but I persuaded him that a limo offered more room to stretch one's legs," said Groucho. "We can swing by your hostelry and scoop you up at twelve-fifteen or thereabouts."

"Hold on a second." I put my hand over the mouthpiece. "Groucho's invited us to go to the fair with him tomorrow."

"We have to deliver that radio script to Banion at McKay and Forman tomorrow afternoon and talk to him about it," she reminded, setting the newspapers on the living room carpet and standing.

"Oh, right, I forgot. I'll tell him we—"

"I can see Banion by myself and you can go along with Groucho," she suggested. "This has something to do with the case, doesn't it?"

"Probably, yeah."

"Then go."

"But I hate to leave you with the job of—"

"I'll have a quick meeting with the ad people and then spend the rest of the afternoon someplace like the Metropolitan Museum," she said.

Into the phone I said, "Jane can't make it, Groucho. But you can pick me up at twelve-fifteen."

"Fine," he said. "I understand that Gypsy Rose Lee is appearing out there and I'll see if she can round up a friend for you."

Twenty-five

I'm only going as far as Queens," I reminded.

"Even so," said Jane, "I think it's my wifely duty to see you off."

We were standing on the midday Manhattan sidewalk in front of the St. Norbert Hotel, awaiting the advent of Groucho and the limousine.

Across the wide street a horse-drawn carriage was just entering Central Park.

"I'll try to bring you back as many World's Fair souvenirs as I can," I promised my wife while scanning the approaching traffic for a sign of Groucho.

"Anything is okay except Trylon and Perisphere salt and pepper shakers," she said.

"Gee, I sort of had my heart set on salt and pepper shakers."

A grey limousine slid to a stop at the curb and the doorman hurried over to open the rear door.

Groucho leaned out. "We've come to collect your husband, Mrs. Denby," he said. "Usually we insist that all contributions be placed in galvanized cans, but we'll waive that rule in your case. And later on we'll be waving the North Dakota state flag."

"Good afternoon, Groucho," said Jane, escorting me over to the long, low car.

"The same to you, my dear," he said as I climbed into the limousine.

I bid good-bye to my wife, pulled the door shut, and the car went gliding away. Groucho's guitar case was sitting on the seat between us. Sniffing at the air, I inquired, "What's that scent?"

"Does it smell like hot pastrami or corned beef?"

I considered. "Pastrami," I decided.

"Then that's me." He patted the guitar case, producing a hollow thump. "I've got two pastrami sandwiches packed in here with my guitar in case of an emergency."

"What if I'd answered corned beef?"

"That's our driver. He's got two corned beef sandwiches in the glove compartment."

"I take it you dropped in at a delicatessen en route."

"I'm under doctor's orders to visit a deli at least once each day." From the pocket of his blazer he withdrew a wrapped bar of halvah and handed it to me. "A small token of my affection."

I took it and slipped it into my jacket pocket. Noticing the glass partition that separated us from our wide-shouldered uniformed driver, I decided we could talk about the case without being overheard. "I've been finding out some stuff about the Manheim business," I said.

"So have I, Rollo, and this pilgrimage to the shrine of Grover Whalen will afford us ample opportunity to compare notes," he said, leaning back in his seat. "The first note I was going to compare was a mash note recently sent to me by Eleanor Roosevelt wherein she confessed an unbridled passion for me. I decided against that, however, since I don't want to provoke your jealousy or envy."

I asked, "First off, what sort of progress is your chum Lieutenant Lewin making?"

"Despite a respect for me that borders on idolatry, Herb Lewin has refrained thus far from confiding much of anything," answered Groucho. "So we're going to have to rely on what we've dug up on our own."

I nodded. "I've lost touch with my best informant out in Los Angeles," I told him. "But before that happened, he told me that the word was that Daniel Manheim was probably involved in the killing of Nick Sanantonio."

"Involved just how?"

"So far the police apparently don't even know about this. But it seems that three freelance out-of-town killers were hired for the job," I said.

"And Manheim did the hiring?" Groucho sat up.

"That's what the consensus is," I said. "And one of the suspected hired killers has been taken care of so far."

"Probably by our friend Vince Salermo."

"Yep."

"We'll get back to gangland in a moment," said Groucho, producing a cigar from his pocket. "Firstly, though, why would Manheim want to get rid of Sanantonio?"

"It could tie in with Dian Bowers."

"Possibly, Rollo, since we know she had an affair with the gambler," said Groucho, unwrapping the stogie and lighting it. "And we also know that Manheim was noted for the violent methods he used in shooing off unwanted suitors of his actresses."

"He had people worked over, but would he go so far as to order somebody murdered?"

"Leo Haskell implied that he would and probably did on one or two prior occasions," said Groucho, exhaling smoke. "But why, specifically, would he want to get rid of Sanantonio?"

I suggested, "Could be Sanantonio didn't want to stop seeing Dian Bowers. Might even be *she* didn't want to stop seeing *him,* huh?"

"She assured me their romance was over."

"That's what *she* says," I pointed out. "A nice girl, sure, but, Groucho, she hasn't been exactly open and truthful with you."

Groucho said, "It could also be that Sanantonio wanted to resume the romance and made it known that he was going to do it openly, with or without Dian's okay. Having his newest star actress linked in the news with a notorious hoodlum wouldn't help *Saint Joan* at all."

"And it sure wouldn't please the people who're Manheim's financial backers, the ones he brought Dian here to Manhattan to meet and impress."

"Sure, a fellow with Manheim's outlook probably wouldn't balk at killing someone if it meant saving a million-dollar movie and an actress worth potentially more than that to him," conceded Groucho. "His moral code was pretty much akin to Salermo's."

"It's a perfect Hollywood motive," I added. "So now, Groucho, let's tentatively assume that Manheim had Sanantonio killed. The next question is—who killed Manheim?"

"Salermo would be high on the list, except for the fact that he apparently didn't know anything about Manheim's involvement in Sanantonio's death until a couple days ago," said Groucho. "Meaning the attempt on Manheim's life on the Super Chief almost certainly couldn't have been arranged by him."

"And we're pretty much convinced that the person who killed Manheim at the Coronet Theater was the same one who made the try on the train."

"Agreed," Groucho said. "Although it could be that the killer had an entirely different reason for killing Manheim, one that has nothing at all to do with Sanantonio."

I asked, "Do you believe that?"

He shook his head and took a puff of his cigar. "Nope. I have a feeling the two killings are tied together."

"So maybe what we have to find is someone who knew Manheim was responsible for Sanantonio's death and killed him out of revenge."

Groucho made a brief shivering motion. "I have to admit that might well be Dian, if she was still in love with Sanantonio," he said ruefully. "Manheim kills her lover, she kills Manheim. A trite situation, but a possible one."

I said, "Sanantonio had other lovers, if revenge is the motive. The list includes Willa Jerome, who was also on the train."

Groucho blew a smoke ring, then watched it dissolve. "Which brings us to Dr. Dowling," he said. "Although it would be too simple if what he wants to tell me is that he has proof that his only patient did Manheim in."

"Dowling didn't say what exactly he wants to talk about?"

"He provided precious few details, Hortense, other than that he'd been brooding about certain events that took place on the Super Chief as it raced across the continent," said Groucho. "Apparently, having come out of one of his drunken stupors, the good doctor starts remembering what went on around him while he was in a soused state."

"And what he's getting vague memories of has something to do with the attempted attack on Manheim?"

"So he implied, although it's possible he merely wants to hear me sing "Lydia the Tattooed Lady" yet again and this is but a flimsy excuse to contact me."

I said, "Willa Jerome is supposed to be a very feisty lady. She might go so far as to murder Manheim for killing her lover."

"She might," agreed Groucho. "That is, if the lady knew for certain he'd ordered the deed done to Sanantonio."

"We don't, as yet, know that she did."

"We'd best strive to find out—and how she might've learned."

"There are some other people we have to learn more about," I reminded. "For instance, there's also Len Cowan, the dancer. His motive would be revenge for the death of his sister."

"A long shot," said Groucho. "But we'd best determine where he was on the night of the Manheim murder."

By this time our limousine was traveling along Grand Central Parkway and we were nearing the fairgrounds.

Twenty-six

The New York World's Fair, which had opened at the end of that April, covered some twelve hundred acres. Its theme was the World of Tomorrow and almost all the many buildings and pavilions had a streamlined, futuristic look. On first arriving at the place, you felt that you'd wandered onto the set of the most expensive science-fiction movie ever made. Part Oz and part the sort of future envisioned in films like *Things to Come*. In fact, H. G. Wells himself had earlier visited the World's Fair and given it his blessing.

There was a great deal of white, but each of the seven distinct zones of the fairgrounds had a specific identifying color that dominated walls, murals, and decorations—red, blue, yellow, and so on. At what was considered the center of things rose the Trylon and Perisphere. A triangular pylon, the Trylon rose up 700 feet in the air beside the 200-feet-in-diameter Perisphere. Both of these structures were stark white and towered over a large lagoon. At the other end of the lagoon stood a 65-foot statue of George Washington. Supposedly the fair was commemorating the 150th anniversary of his inauguration.

Several years in the making, the fair included exhibits from thirty-some states and nearly sixty countries—including Italy and Russia but not Germany. There were vast modern buildings devoted to such outfits as Ford, General Electric, DuPont, Heinz, Wonder Bread, and RCA. You could see a demonstration of television, watch cows being milked by machines, see Eleanor Holm and Johnny Weismuller swim, talk to a robot, and get an idea of what an ideal city would look like in 1960. There was an abundance of outdoor artwork, with huge statues and murals. A Greek god here, a husky workingman there, a water nymph guarding a fountain. Trees, shrubs, and hedges flourished everywhere.

The president of the World's Fair, and its most active publicist, was a stocky moustached fellow named Grover Whalen. A former Manhattan police chief and later the city's official greeter from the 1920s on, Whalen even provided special transportation and a personal guide around the fairgrounds for Groucho and me.

A slim red-haired young woman, clad in the tan uniform of an official guide—complete with the Trylon and Perisphere patch on the left sleeve—approached our limousine as it pulled to a stop in the Special Visitors section of the vast parking lot. "Mr. Marx?" she inquired uncertainly as he came slumping out of the backseat.

"To the best of my knowledge, I am. Although there's been some talk to the effect that I am actually the lost dauphin of France." He took hold of her hand, bent to kiss it.

She tugged her hand free before his lips made contact. "I wasn't immediately certain, because I guess you use a lot of makeup in the movies," she said, "and it must hide most of those wrinkles."

"Wrinkles, my dear? Why, I'm noted in Hollywood for my smooth, unruffled skin," he told her. "Out there I'm often alluded to as that baby's bottom with a moustache."

I said, "I'm Frank Denby, miss."

"Oh, and I'm Peggy Kurtin," the girl said. "Mr. Whalen's office sent me over to welcome you and Mr. Marx, give you a brief tour of the fair, and then deliver you to the Bascom Music Pavilion."

"A few laugh wrinkles around the eyes maybe," Groucho was muttering. "But that's due to the fact that I'm such a merry, fun-loving fellow."

"You also have a moustache usually," added Peggy, beckoning us to follow her.

"I lost everything in the Depression," he said.

The uniformed guide led us to a sort of cart that was pulled by a small electric tractor. "Climb aboard, gentlemen," she invited, standing aside. After Groucho and I had taken the rear seats in the open cart, she sat in the front seat. "You can start now, Alex."

"Right you are, Peg." The driver was young, blonde, and sun-tanned.

"We'll swing by the Trylon and Perisphere and then cut over to the entertainment area, Mr. Marx," Peggy explained.

Groucho took out a cigar. "How'd you end up in this racket, sister?"

"I came to New York exactly a year ago to break into the theater," she said with a slight shrug. "I'm still waiting, so when I heard they were looking for pretty girls to work here at the World's Fair, I tried out."

We crossed something called the Bridge of Wings and moved toward the symbolic center of the fair. The afternoon was warm, the sky cloudless, and hundreds of people were roaming the tree-lined streets.

"This is an exceptionally clean locale, Rollo," observed Groucho.

"We keep it spotless," said Peggy.

"I've always been partial to a few spots here and there," said Groucho. "Especially on leopards and polka-dot bow ties."

"There's the Westinghouse Building over there on the right," Peggy pointed out. "That's where you can see Elektro the robot."

"Too bad we don't have a leftover brother," said Groucho, lighting his cigar. "We could call him Elektro Marx."

"If you have any time after the performance," Peggy told us, "I can escort you through the Democracity exhibit inside the Perisphere. It's a diorama that shows what an ideal planned community will look like in the future."

"Good thing this isn't Europe," said Groucho. "The chief ingredient of the communities of the future over there will be rubble."

"I think you have to have a positive attitude about the future, Mr. Marx. The underlying notion of this whole fair is optimism about tomorrow."

"Hitler's idea of what constitutes the World of Tomorrow and the fair's differ somewhat," he said. "I hear that Grover Whalen and his pal Mussolini also think Hitler has some dandy notions."

"I know people say nasty things about Mr. Whalen behind his back, but—"

"It's a pretty wide back, kiddo. There's a lot of room behind there for making nasty remarks."

"Well, he's a very personable man and he did more for the New York World's Fair than just about anybody."

Groucho nodded. "He did a lot for Red-baiting back a couple decades ago, too."

Peggy looked back at him, a frown on her face. "You're not as cheerful as I imagined you'd be."

"I'm not even as cheerful as I imagined I'd be," he replied, exhaling smoke.

After circling the imposing Trylon and Perisphere, we headed back toward the entertainment area.

We were rolling along toward the Empire State Bridge and Liberty Lake, when a group of fair visitors started emerging from the General Electric building and spotted Groucho. "It's Groucho Marx," yelled a fat man in a double-breasted blue suit. "Groucho. Hey, Groucho," shouted a freckled teenager. "Is that one of the Marx Brothers?" cried another. "Groucho! Groucho!" called several.

"Lepers met with a similar reception in the Middle Ages," observed Groucho, casually thumbing his nose at the small crowd.

Our electric wagon slowed as a good two dozen tourists came spilling out into the street. Before they were directly in our path, the wagon halted.

Peggy inquired, "Do you wish me to shoo them away, Mr. Marx?"

"No, my child. As one of the leading intellectuals of our era, I'm often being pestered by my disciples and I feel it's my obligation to toss a few pearls of wisdom their way," he told our guide. "Stop and I'll radiate for a few minutes."

"Hi, Groucho," greeted the freckled teenager, stopping about three feet from us and grinning.

A woman with a box camera asked, "Would you object to a group photo?"

"Depends on what group you have in mind," he said. "I'm sort of partial to the Mills Brothers right now, though I'd settle for a nice shot of Phil Napoleon and His Emperors of Jazz. However, if you prefer a smaller group, we can lie in wait until Kate Smith comes ankling by."

The woman chuckled. "Mr. Marx, you're incorrigible."

"Alas, unfortunately, I am," he admitted ruefully. "To be frank, I haven't been corriged for many a moon." He leaned and tapped my knee. "Forgive me for being Frank, when you already are."

The teenager asked, "Which is your favorite Marx Brothers movie?"

"I only have to be in the things," explained Groucho. "I don't have to like them."

A thin woman in a flowered dress eased closer. "My son impersonated you in a talent show and won twenty-five dollars."

"So where's my split?"

"Oh, you're such a clown."

"A clown, is it? When's the last time a clown asked you for twelve-fifty?"

A man asked, "Are you going to be appearing at the fair at all, Mr. Marx?"

"I am appearing this very afternoon, sir," he informed him. "We're doing an informal version of *The Mikado* at the Bascom Music Pavilion at two-thirty."

"Wonderful. We don't want to miss that."

Another man said, "I saw you and your brothers in vaudeville."

"Fortunately there's a statute of limitations in this case, so it's too late to get your money back."

Coughing, Peggy tapped her wristwatch.

Groucho said, "My friends, I must be going. I only have time to sing a few verses of "Lydia the Tattooed Lady," the hit tune from my upcoming cinematic triumph *At the Circus*. Then I must rush off to the pavilion, where I'm certain a few choice seats are still available."

Peggy signaled our driver to start moving again when Groucho was about halfway through the song.

Twenty-seven

When we went rolling past the Marine Amphitheatre, where Billy Rose's *Aquacade* was being staged daily, Peggy announced, "There's the Bascom Music Pavilion up ahead, Mr. Marx, just this side of the Terrace Club."

"I was hoping we'd be working closer to the *Strange As It Seems* freak museum," he complained, "so I might drop in and see if they were hiring."

"You might want to see the *Aquacade* swim show later," our guide suggested. "It's really marvelous."

"I try to stay clear of Johnny Weismuller, since the lad is insanely jealous of me."

"Why would that be?"

"He saw me once at Malibu while I was wearing leopard-skin trunks and he's been fearful of losing his Tarzan job ever since," explained Groucho as our cart came to a stop beside the pavilion. "As soon as I perfect my jungle yell, I'm going to approach Louis B. Mayer about assuming the role."

"There might be some chimpanzee openings right now," said Peggy, stepping down from the cart.

"Ah, the cruel barbs of youth." Groucho disembarked and I followed.

"There's a sign taped to the stage door entrance," I noticed.

"So there is, Rollo." Groucho went loping over to the door.

The sign read, "*Mikado* rehearsal postponed until 4:30 P.M. Backstage area will open at 3:00."

"Darn, things like this are always happening, Mr. Marx," said Peggy apologetically. "I wasn't told about it, sorry. Would you like me to take you and Mr. Denby to a restaurant for a snack while you're waiting?"

Groucho hefted his guitar case. "I had the foresight to bring lunch, my dear."

"Well, I can show you around some more if you'd like," she offered. "I can't simply abandon you here."

"I'm frequently abandoned," he said. "Still and all, I'd be delighted to have you act as our Virgil through this art deco inferno."

"How about you, Mr. Denby?"

"Think I'd rather roam around on my own," I said. "I want to pick up some souvenirs for my wife. Suppose, Groucho, I meet you back here at around three?"

He said, "I don't know if Peggy trusts herself alone with me."

She smiled. "It's okay, Mr. Marx. Alex is very good at handling mashers."

"I feared as much." He went slouching back to the cart. "I'll see you anon, Rollo."

As Jane stepped clear of the shower stall, she heard the telephone ringing. Tugging on a white terry-cloth robe, she barefooted to the phone that sat next to the bed. "Hello?"

A desk clerk said in a polite, nasal voice, "Mrs. Denby, we have a collect long-distance telephone call for your husband. It's from Los Angeles, California."

"Who's calling?"

"His name is . . . it seems to be Tim O'Hara."

"Might it be Tim O'Hearn?"

"Yes, that's likely it. Is your husband willing to accept the call?"

"Frank isn't here just now, but he's been trying to get in touch with Mr. O'Hearn for quite some time," said Jane, noticing that she'd left damp footprints on the bedroom's thick flowered carpet. "Tell Mr. O'Hearn that I can talk to him and pass along the information to my husband."

"Very well, Mrs. Denby."

After a moment O'Hearn inquired, "Who is this again?"

"Jane Denby."

"I thought Frank's wife was named Jane Danner."

"Same person. Jane Danner's my professional name. Frank's been trying to get hold of you since—"

"I was sick and I got worse," explained my informant. "I had to go to the damn clinic and they kept me there almost a whole afternoon, Jane."

"You're okay now?"

He coughed a dry cough, then wheezed. "Well, my chest is always weak and when I come down with a cold, it's worse," he said. "But, yeah, I guess I'm better than I was. I'm not so dizzy now and the fever's gone."

"That's good," she told him. "So what have you found out about—"

"I suppose I can trust you."

"Frank does."

"You draw for the funny papers, huh?"

"I do, yes. What have you—"

"Did Frank explain to you he was going to wire me another twenty bucks?"

"When you came through with more information."

"So can you get that dough off to me the next couple hours, Jane? They got me taking some cough medicine that costs an arm and a leg."

"I can wire you the money, yes. Tell me what—"

O'Hearn coughed again. "I found out why Manheim got so riled up about Nick Sanantonio," he confided. "Seems like, after Sanantonio quit hanging around with Willa Jerome, he decided to get back with this Dian Bowers."

"I see." Jane had started making notes on a sheet of hotel stationery with a fountain pen of mine she'd found next to the table lamp.

"Dian wasn't, so I hear, especially interested in that, but Sanantonio threatened to tell the papers about their romance unless she gave in and took up with him again," continued O'Hearn. "The guy was even aiming to follow her to New York and crash her meetings with the reporters."

"That would've messed up Manheim's plans considerably."

"You're not kidding. And that's the reason, according to the way I hear it, that Manheim arranged to have Sanantonio taken care of."

Jane asked, "And did Salermo, in turn, have Manheim taken care of?"

"He would've, but somebody beat him to the punch."

"Anything else I should pass on to Frank?"

"Well, I've also been hearing that Willa Jerome was still carrying a pretty big torch for Sanantonio. She was figuring to win him back from the Bowers dame—but then he got rubbed out," said the informant.

"She might want to get revenge on the man who killed her boyfriend and ruined her plans," said Jane. "Thing is—did Willa know Manheim was responsible for having Sanantonio killed? And if so, how the heck did she find out before Salermo and his boys did?"

"I don't have all the details on that yet, Mrs. Denby, but it looks like she did."

"Knew about it before she boarded the Super Chief last Friday night?"

"That's the way it's shaping up, yeah."

"Anything more?"

"That's about it for now," said O'Hearn, coughing again. "I'll get back to you folks soon as I find out anything else."

"Well, thanks a lot. I'm sure Frank will—"

"And my money?"

"It'll be winging its way to you soon as I get to the nearest telegraph office," she promised.

"I appreciate it, ma'am," said O'Hearn. "And let me tell you, much as I like Frank, you're sure a lot easier to do business with."

Twenty-eight

Strolling the fairgrounds, I decided I'd like to take a look at the robot our guide had mentioned. Making my way through the afternoon crowds, I crossed the short, arching Empire State Bridge and made my way to the Commerce Circle.

The Westinghouse Building loomed up across the way from the General Electric Building, which had an immense stainless-steel bolt of lightning striking its roof. Westinghouse had worked up considerable publicity with their Time Capsule. It was a torpedo-shaped container they'd buried some fifty feet down in what they were labeling the Immortal Well. The capsule was stuffed with everyday artifacts of life in 1939 plus several million pages of microfilm. The thing wasn't due to be dug up and unpacked until the year 6839.

It was sunk in the courtyard in front of the streamlined, futuristic building. As I passed by the site and the thirty-some visitors gathered around under the circular metal canopy with THE TIME CAPSULE etched around it, I got a sudden unsettling intimation of my own mortality. I realized that I'd be dead and gone thousands of years before anybody unearthed the capsule. New York might be long gone as well by then.

After nearly bumping into a bunch of ogling sailors, I went inside. It took a few minutes to find my way to the Hall of Electrical Living, where Elektro the robot was on display. He was up on an elevated stand, a railing around him. Elektro was about eight feet tall, a glistening metallic fellow who looked like a cross between an animated furnace and the Tin Woodman of Oz. The robots to be seen on the covers of pulp fiction magazines were most often sinister lads, with a fondness for carrying off sparsely clad young women. But Elektro seemed to be an amiable, if somewhat clunky, mechanical man.

As I stood watching in the small circling crowd, he sang a little song, spoke a few sentences in a rumbling tinny voice, counted to ten on his long metal fingers, and played with his small robot dog, who we were told was named Sparko. Electro also gave a demonstration of his ability to sweep floors—Westinghouse apparently was hoping for a future that included mechanical servants in every middle-class American home.

Not convinced I'd want a giant robot lumbering around our place, I enjoyed the demonstration anyway. I didn't look toward the Time Capsule on my way out and headed back in the direction of the entertainment area.

At a book and magazine kiosk between the Macy's and Gimbel's buildings on World's Fair Boulevard, I noticed a copy of *New York World's Fair Comics* on sale. It contained Superman, plus some other characters I'd never heard of, including a magician named Zatara and a mysterious fellow who wore a gas mask and called himself The Sandman. It sold for two bits and I figured it would make a nice souvenir for Jane. She'd been picking up an occasional comic book off the newsstands lately and there'd already been some talk about reprinting *Hollywood Molly* in that format.

On Orange Blossom Lane, still a good half mile from the Bascom Music Pavilion, I came upon a small theater named the Little Broadway. It had a big, bright poster tacked up on one of its walls next to the closed ticket booth. The poster announced, "Opening Tonite! Jitterbug Follies! With Ella May Keaton, Andy Sherriff, Len Cowan, and 24 Gorgeous Rug-Cutters!"

Len Cowan was the angry dancer who'd had a grudge against Manheim.

I was standing there reflecting on that fact when somebody suddenly pushed me hard in the back. I went slamming into the wall.

"I'm tired of you bastards spying on me."

Groucho leaned back on the tan-colored bench, spread his guitar case across his knees, and opened it. As he withdrew the second pastrami sandwich, he asked Peggy, "You're absolutely certain, my child, that you won't share my humble repast?"

Nose wrinkling slightly, the young guide said, "No thank you, Mr. Marx."

The cart was parked beside the grassy glade, Alex standing beside it gazing in the direction of the towering Pylon.

Snapping the case shut, Groucho rested it on the ground next to the bench. He unwrapped the sandwich, took a bite, and then picked up the guidebook that rested on the seat beside him. "I want, once again, to thank you *and* Mr. Whalen for presenting this handsome book to me," he said, chewing. "*Official Guidebook Twenty-Five Cents.* I'm most grateful."

"We do it for most of our celebrities," answered Peggy, who was sitting as far from him on the bench as she could without actually falling off. "Are there any further attractions you'd like to visit before we take you back to the music pavilion?"

"Well, let's see. We've already visited such illuminating sites as the Infant Incubator Building, Frank Buck's Jungleland—complete with thirty Malays and twenty-five seals—the Boy Scout Camp, and Salvador Dali's Dream of Venus." He sighed. "My sense of wonder probably can't take much more." He began leafing through the pages of the thick paper-covered book as he ate. "Ah, how about the Timken Roller Bearing Company? We can actually see, so they say, 'a mechanical display of the elements that go into a hundred pounds of alloy steel.' That'd be something." He shut the guidebook and concentrated on his sandwich for a moment. "I'm also torn between Nature's Mistakes and George Jessel. Although I can see more than enough of Jessel in Los Angeles, if not in this context."

"Mr. Jessel doesn't actually appear in the Old New York show every day," Peggy pointed out. "He supervises the entertainment that—"

"Next thing you'll be telling me that Gypsy Rose Lee doesn't appear in her show and then I won't have anything to look forward to."

"No, you can see her perform her striptease tonight if you'd care to."

Out on the wide sunny roadway a Greyhound Bus jerked to a halt opposite to Groucho's bench. The front door hissed open and the uniformed driver called out, "Hey, some of my passengers say you're Groucho Marx."

Groucho jumped to his feet, glaring. "How dare you call me that?" he demanded, grabbing up his guitar case and striding up close to the stopped bus.

"Well, are you?"

"Alas, no. I'm merely Groucho Marx's stand-in."

There were about twenty passengers inside the bus and they'd all moved to the windows on Groucho's side.

A plump woman tugged her window open. "Groucho Marx doesn't use a stand-in," she stated.

"Then who do you think does all that horseback riding stuff, madam?"

"He doesn't ride a horse in his movies," said a skinny teenage boy.

"He doesn't?" Groucho gave a puzzled shrug. "Then it could be I'm the stand-in for Bob Nolan and the Sons of the Pioneers instead."

"Can we have your autograph, Mr. Marx?" requested a slim young woman from another window.

"Why certainly, my dear." He whipped out a pen and inscribed his name on the side of the bus. "And now, to speed you on your way, I'll sing you the complete lyrics of "Lydia the Tattooed Lady," the hit tune from the forthcoming Marx Brothers epic, *At the Circus*."

"We're running behind schedule already, Mr. Marx. Sorry." The driver shut the door, the passengers waved good-bye, and the bus went rumbling away.

Shoulders hunched dejectedly, Groucho carried his guitar case back to the bench. "It's difficult to hold an audience when they're on wheels," he told Peggy.

She checked her wristwatch again. "We'd best be heading back anyway, Mr. Marx."

As their cart was passing by one of the many splashing fountains, they noticed a small crowd gathering at the edge of the water. Two husky uniformed World's Fair police officers were wading into the fountain.

"Something's amiss," said Groucho.

"We can take a look." Alex stopped the cart.

Peggy and Groucho climbed down and moved to the edge of the fountain.

"He's dead," said a dark-haired woman. "I just bet that poor man's dead."

"He's dead sure enough," seconded a gaunt man in a tan suit and Panama hat.

"Is he dead?" asked a ten-year old boy.

"Stand back, folks," ordered one of the cops. "We're going to try to use artificial respiration on this man."

"You're not going to revive that guy," said a young sailor, pointing out the dripping body of the plump middle-aged man. "See—he's been stabbed in the back."

"Damn," said Groucho quietly. "Too late."

Peggy frowned at him, puzzled. "Do you know him?"

"Yes, that's Dr. Dowling," he answered. "He thought he had something important to tell me."

Twenty-nine

Spinning around, after I'd detached myself from the *Jitterbug Follies* poster, I found I was facing Len Cowan in person.

"Nosy asshole," he accused, starting to throw a punch at me.

I sidestepped, caught the dancer's fist, and twisted his arm up behind his back. "Neither Groucho Marx nor I have been trailing you," I assured him as I shoved him against the ticket booth. "Encountering you here and now was a coincidence. However, we would like to have a chat with you."

"Take a flying leap for yourself," he said, wincing.

"You're better trained for that sort of thing," I said. "Look, the New York City police are probably going to be coming to talk to you. Why not talk to me first and, maybe, save yourself some trouble?"

"How? By talking to two morons instead of one?"

"Groucho happens to be a friend of the cop investigating the Manheim killing," I told him. "He might be able to put in a good word for you." I had no idea if that was possible, but I was hoping it sounded plausible.

After a few seconds, Len said, "Okay, all right. Let go of me, Denby, and we can talk."

Watchful, I relaxed my hold on him and stepped back. "You had an argument with Manheim, in front of witnesses," I reminded. "You were on the Super Chief when somebody attacked him and his bodyguard. Furthermore, you were in the New York area when Manheim was murdered at the Coronet."

"Sure, and I was in Ford's Theater the night Lincoln was shot." Folding his arms, Len leaned back against the theater wall just to the left of the big yellow and red poster.

"Motive and opportunity," I said. "You had both."

"You know, both you and your Marx Brothers partner are saps," he observed. "Otherwise you'd have found out that it wasn't me who tried to kill Manheim on the train. It was a . . . well, hell, you're supposed to be detectives. You find out."

I stepped closer to him. "It was a *what*?"

The young dancer gave a lazy shrug. "That mysterious dark figure Groucho saw was a woman."

"Oh, so? Groucho said the figure was wearing pants, a jacket, and—"

"Didn't you ever see a dame wear pants and dress like a guy? Hell, go to a Marlene Dietrich movie sometime."

I asked, "How do you *know* it was a woman?"

He sighed and I could smell the couple of whiskeys he'd had earlier. "I saw her."

"You saw her? Then why in the hell didn't you tell somebody?"

He grinned. "At the time I had no idea what had happened," he explained. "I was walking along a corridor on the damn train. This figure came running toward me, shined a flashlight in my face, and shoved me out of the way. Then she ran on out of the car."

"But you saw her?"

"Not to identify, not a face," he said. "But I *felt* her as she pushed by and, believe me, it was a woman."

"Any idea who?"

He shrugged again. "Not really, no."

"And why didn't you say anything afterwards, when you found out what had happened?"

He laughed now. "Don't be a jerk," he said. "Anybody who was trying to kill Manheim, that was okay with me. I'm glad she finally succeeded. He was a miserable son of a bitch and if somebody'd knocked him off earlier, my sister would still be alive."

I said, "That's an interesting yarn, Cowan. If it's true then—"

"It's true," he assured me. "Although I might forget it all if I was hauled into court to testify."

"Any stories about last Tuesday night, when Manheim was murdered?"

"If I need to, I can come up with an alibi for the whole evening," he said. "And you don't have to take my word at all, Denby. Just ask your friend May Sankowitz."

"You were with May?"

He nodded, grinning. "Took her to dinner," he said, "then spent the whole night with her. Ask."

I said, "If I have to."

"Come and see our show sometime, and bring that cute wife of yours," he invited, giving me a mock salute. He went walking off.

There were four uniformed World's Fair cops beside the fountain now. Their outfits were similar to those of highway patrolmen. A thickset blonde officer was on one knee beside the sprawled body of Dr. Dowling. Gingerly, he extracted the dead man's wallet from the breast pocket of his soggy suit coat.

It dripped water as he opened it. After a moment he handed it to a dark-haired officer standing at the fountain edge. "His driver's license says he's Philip Dowling, an MD from out in Los Angeles, California," he said.

After glancing at the wallet, the dark-haired cop looked around at the growing gathering of curious fairgoers. "Anybody know this man?"

Peggy nudged Groucho, whispering, "Aren't you going to speak up?"

"They already have his name and address, my dear," he answered quietly. "And if I get tangled up in the law's delay, *The Mikado* will go on without a Lord High Executioner."

"Doesn't your civic duty come before show business?"

"You ask me that, a young lady who ran away from home to go into show business herself?"

"Okay, don't get involved," said Peggy. "Still I feel that—"

"I saw the guy tumble into the fountain," volunteered one of the sailors in the crowd.

The dark cop asked, "Did you see who attacked him?"

"He was by himself when I spotted the guy," answered the sailor. "He came weaving along, staggering some. Then he stumbled and fell over into the fountain with a big splash."

Another sailor added, "We were about to go in and yank him out when one of your boys came along and told us to stand back."

The patrolman asked them, "Did you notice where he was coming from?"

They shook their heads, but a plump woman in a flowered dress said, "I saw him a little while ago over that way." She pointed. "Over there, where that row of saloons and cocktail bars is. I think he was coming out of one of them and he was staggering. I assumed he'd had a few too many."

"Was he with anyone?"

"No, Officer," answered the woman. "He was entirely alone."

Groucho eased back from the crowd, gesturing to Peggy to come along. "Before we head for the wicked stage," he said, "let's frequent yonder saloons."

"For a drink?"

"Nope. For information."

Thirty

The office of the Bascom Music Pavilion was painted eggshell white and had a mural all across one windowless wall. The mural depicted, in a style that mixed elements of Diego Rivera, Rockwell Kent, and Rube Goldberg, the high points in the history of the Bascom organization. From the clues the bright-colored painting provided, I deduced that Bascom had spent most of the century manufacturing musical instruments and employing a lot of very muscular guys who were fond of showing up for work without their shirts.

I reflected on the possible history of the company while I sat on the edge of the oaken desk in the unoccupied office and waited for my call to Manhattan to go through.

When I'd returned to the pavilion, ahead of Groucho, the backstage doorman who let me in told me that my wife wanted me to get in touch with her.

After about five minutes on the phone, I was able to reach her. "How'd the meeting with the network go?" I asked.

"It was postponed, Frank. But that's not why I—"

"Postponed—how come?"

"That doesn't happen to be one of the pieces of information anybody bothered to convey to me, dear," answered Jane. "All I know is that it's rescheduled for tomorrow at two-thirty. Now, as to the reason I telephoned you out there at—"

"You mean this isn't a simple romantic gesture? Something along the lines of 'I had to hear your voice, my darling.' "

"That, too, sweetie pie. But O'Hearn telephoned and gave me some information for you."

"Where the devil's he been?"

"Ailing apparently and visiting a clinic," Jane said. "I thought you'd want to hear what he dug up. Oh, by the way, how did *The Mikado* go?"

"Postponed, until later today."

She gave me an account of what Tim O'Hearn had told her.

Groucho looked from his makeup mirror to me and back to the mirror again. "Even though this is an informal rehearsal we're staging for the myriad of my devoted fans who are pouring into this temple of the lively arts," he said, "I feel obliged to daub on my greasepaint moustache and eyebrows. Otherwise they might mistake me for Ronald Colman and demand their money back."

"Soon as your performance is finished, we've got to talk over the whole case again," I told him from the rickety chair near the table. "There sure as hell have been some new developments." We'd already talked about what had been happening, including Dr. Dowling's murder and Len Cowan's telling me it was a woman who tried to kill Manheim on the train east. I'd also recapped what O'Hearn had passed along about Sanantonio's attempting to woo Dian again and the fact that Willa Jerome had still been carrying a torch for the gangster.

"All very interesting developments, yes. Particularly the probable sex of the probable killer," said Groucho. "And it occurs to me that that's the kind of sex I often have, probable."

I nodded, asking, "Is Peggy Kurtin still hereabouts anywhere?"

"She and her accompanying lout will return in a few moments to watch me render *The Mikado*. Why do you ask, Rollo?"

"She ought to be able to get us a copy of Willa Jerome's itinerary here at the fair today," I replied.

"Yes, we must, among other things, pay that lady a visit of condolence."

Someone tapped on the dressing room door. "We'll be starting in five minutes, Mr. Marx."

After examining his makeup one more time, Groucho stood up and away from the mirror. "If I'm the hit I expect to be in *The Mikado*, just think of all the other Gilbert and Sullivan works there are to do."

The standing ovation he received at the conclusion of the informal rehearsal of *The Mikado* prompted Groucho to offer the enthusiastic World's Fair audience an encore. That consisted of a rendition of "Lydia the Tattooed Lady," accompanied on his guitar, plus a medley of favorites from earlier Marx Brothers movies. For an encore to the encore Groucho did some of his eccentric dancing and then, for reasons he could not later explain, he sat on the edge of the stage to sing "Mexicali Rose" and "Birmingham Jail."

By the time he was back in his dressing room, taking off his greasepaint, it was a few minutes after seven o'clock. And by the time he finished giving a mass interview to five reporters and a World's Fair publicist, it was past seven-thirty.

"Forgive me, Rollo," he apologized when we were alone. "Sometimes my doggoned career gets in the way of my sleuthing."

I said, "According to the list Peggy turned up for me, Willa Jerome will be having her final press conference at the British Pavilion, public cordially invited, at eight-thirty. So we've got time to catch up with her and pay a social call."

"While I was waiting backstage between entrances," Groucho said, turning his chair so that he was facing me and leaning both his elbows back on the makeup table, "I thought quite a lot about this whole case."

"I've been thinking about it, too."

"Here's what I've concluded," said Groucho. "See if our speculations match, Rollo." Rising, he commenced pacing the small dressing room. "All right, it starts in Los Angeles. Nick Sanantonio, famed mobster, gambler, and ladies' man, decides he wants to rekindle his once-blooming romance with Dian Bowers—once known as sweet and innocent Nancy Washburn."

"You're assuming she was sweet and innocent, Groucho. But for all we know she was two-timing Washburn long before she ever met Sanantonio."

"True," he conceded. "I'm a notoriously bad judge of women. I once dated Typhoid Mary and thought she was in perfect health. But back to the matter at hand." He located a cigar in the pocket of his blazer. "Sanantonio tells our Dian that he wants back in the ball game. She's not too charmed by the idea and tries to discourage the goniff. He, however, persists. A man with a reputation for getting exactly what he wants, Sanantonio makes it known that he's going to make considerable trouble unless he gets Dian back." Groucho unwrapped the cigar. "He'll make trouble for her *and* for her budding career. He'll start a scandal by announcing that he's been her lover. The fact that she's been a gangster's tootsie will not only sabotage her as a potential movie star, but it'll probably wipe out the chances of *Saint Joan* at the box office. Dian will be out of work and Manheim stands to lose several million bucks. The public won't buy a woman who's been sleeping around with thugs as Joan of Arc."

"And thus Sanantonio would've caused a disaster for Manheim."

"Which gave him his motive for having Sanantonio removed from the scene," picked up Groucho. "To cover his tracks he rigs up the killing to look like a typical, everyday gangland rubout."

"He fooled the police, and probably Dian Bowers," I said. "But Salermo didn't buy it and, it seems certain, neither did Willa Jerome."

"It's my conclusion that Willa killed Manheim because he murdered her lover," said Groucho. "Even though the lad had abandoned her, she was planning to win him back. His being dead spoiled that scheme and left her thinking of revenge." He paused, lit his cigar, and exhaled smoke. "The necktie, my boy."

"Beg pardon?"

"It only occurred to me while I was in the wings earlier, but you recounted to me a remark that Willa made aboard the Super Chief," said Groucho. "She commented on the gaudy red tie Arneson was wearing. Yet—"

"That's right, when she saw him at the Mexican joint and later on the train, he was wearing that tropical number," I realized. "He didn't change ties until much later."

"And she wouldn't have seen the red tie unless she'd encountered him in the vicinity of Manheim's bedroom and happened to notice the tie after she'd knocked him out and shined her flashlight on him."

"Not courtroom evidence," I mentioned, "but convincing nonetheless, Groucho."

He took a thoughtful puff on his cigar. "We still don't know how Willa found out that Manheim was behind the murder of her lover, though."

"For now, we just have to assume that she did," I said. "She, with or without the help of Emily Collinson, her secretary, worked out a way to kill Manheim on the train. When that didn't work, she tried again in New York."

"We know she was backstage at the Coronet during the dress rehearsal of *Make Mine Murder*. So she would have seen the dummy corpse being set to fall out on the stage—and her dramatic flair inspired her to consider doing the same thing to Manheim if she had the chance."

"And she had the chance the next night when she trailed him to the theater and overheard his fracas with Washburn."

Rubbing his hands together, Groucho said, "I think we've got a plausible scenario here, my boy."

I said, "It seems likely that Dr. Dowling noticed something while he was traveling with Willa and Emily in his usual drunken stupor. He started to remember details and phoned you and, when Willa got wind of it, she took care of him, too."

Groucho said, "The only little flaw in this is that we have to figure out a way to persuade Willa to confess. Because what we have thus far is an interesting story, but—"

Someone knocked on the door. "Mr. Marx, are you still in there?"

Groucho started for the door. "They're probably going to charge me for keeping my light burning."

The doorman was out there with a note in a pale blue envelope. "This was left for you about a half hour ago by a delivery boy, sir."

Groucho accepted the note and shut the door. "Could be a declaration of undying love from Gypsy Rose Lee," he speculated, opening it. "But, no, it's a hasty note from Emily Collinson."

"Saying?"

Groucho cleared his throat. " 'Mr. Marx: You have to help me. I realize that I've made a terrible mistake. I should have spoken about the terrible things Willa was doing long before this. Now it may be too late, but I'm hoping you can help me. I'm afraid she's going to kill me next, the way she did poor Phil Dowling. I'm hiding in the shut-down Haunted House Arcade. Come in the back entrance. I know you and Mr. Denby have experience with murderers and, please, you must come and help me get away safely. Emily Collinson.' "

"A damsel in distress," I said.

"So we're led to believe." He put the letter back in its envelope, stuck the envelope in his jacket pocket. "We'd best ride to the rescue."

Thirty-one

Night had fallen on the World's Fair and all across the dark sky there were scrawls of bright-colored light, geysers of illuminated water, and splashes of gold, crimson, and electric blue. Music, noise, and laughter were thick.

Groucho and I left much of that behind when we turned off onto a side lane that ran from the picnic grounds toward Liberty Lake. The Haunted House Arcade sat darkly next to a boarded-up shooting gallery. It had been built to look like the sort of haunted Victorian mansion you'd see in a Universal horror movie. Like a few of the other 1939 concessions, it hadn't thrived. Shut down, it sat awaiting an optimistic new tenant who'd revise, renovate, or change it completely.

There were only a few overhead streetlights down this way and the thick shadows seemed to muffle the noise of the fairgrounds we'd left behind.

"That reminds me," said Groucho as we neared the haunted house, "Bela Lugosi didn't send me a Christmas card last year. I wonder if he's miffed at us because Harpo tried to drive a stake through his heart at that party in Malibu."

"Some vampires do carry grudges."

"Ain't it the truth?" said Groucho. "And zombies can be even worse. I dated a girl in New Orleans once who . . . Ah, but, Rollo, we're at the back door to this gloomy establishment."

I took hold of the brass doorknob in the ornately carved oaken door and turned. With a spectral creak the door swung open inward.

Groucho clicked on the small pocket flashlight he'd brought along. "I've got to cease packing this in my guitar case," he decided. "It's starting to smell too much like a pastrami sandwich. Although, I suppose, that's not all bad."

Shutting the creaking door behind us, we moved quietly along the shadowy hallway. Artificial cobwebs festooned the wrought-iron wall lamps and the crystal chandeliers and shrouded the claw-footed chairs that were lined up along the dark-paneled walls.

There were several plastic bats stacked under one of the chairs, along with a yellowed plastic skull.

Our footfalls caused real dust to swirl up.

"Footprints," observed Groucho, pointing with his flash beam. "Two people up ahead of us."

"Both of them women."

"If you'll be so kind as to step in here, gents," suggested a female voice on our left.

"The correct line," observed Groucho, "is 'won't you step into my parlor?' "

A portable electric lantern was turned on in the parlor and we could see Willa Jerome framed in the doorway. She was holding a .32 snub-nose revolver and wearing dark slacks and a navy blue pullover.

"Ah, good evening, Miss Jerome." Groucho bowed slightly. "I'm a great fan of yours and I was wondering if I sent you two bits, would you send me an autographed photograph of yourself in a glamourous pose?"

"In here, both of you," ordered the actress, gesturing with the gun.

After we crossed the threshold, Emily Collinson came up and frisked us. She took Groucho's flashlight and my pocketknife.

"You can continue to fondle me, if you'd like," he invited the secretary.

"Asshole," she said.

"Now, now, young woman, that's no way to address one of the two stalwart champions who rushed out into the night to save you from a dire fate," said Groucho.

"Two jerks, you mean." Emily tossed the flashlight onto a bentwood love seat, where a full-size plastic skeleton was sprawled. "You just dote on rescuing poor girls in trouble, like that insipid bitch who calls herself Dian Bowers."

I asked Willa, "Now what?"

"You'll be found here, eventually," she answered. "Two more unfortunate victims of the crazed killer who murdered poor Phil Dowling."

"Also poor Daniel Manheim," added Groucho.

The actress nodded, smiling. "If Phil hadn't started remembering things *and* having pangs of conscience, he'd certainly be alive still," she said. "He wasn't, when he was sober, a bad doctor and we'll miss him. He was especially good at prescribing all sorts of useful drugs and medications for me and my friends."

"He was actually known to have sober moments?" Groucho's eyebrows rose.

"You're taking up too much time," said Emily, impatient.

"You really don't think," I put in, "that you can murder Groucho Marx and not get caught?"

"Daniel Manheim's dead and we're still free," reminded Willa. "He was—forgive me, Groucho—a lot more bloody famous than you'll ever be."

"Probably, though nowhere near as cute."

I asked them, "Why are you adding us to your list?"

Emily said, "We warned you to drop this on the damn train. You didn't pay any attention."

Willa said, "Once Phil Dowling made an appointment to talk to you and then got killed before he could—well, it would only have been a matter of time before you connected us with the Manheim execution."

"Killing you right now," added Emily, "means you're not going to keep poking around in our business."

"True, death is a great deterrent," agreed Groucho. "Since we're scheduled for immediate shipment for glory and will probably be rotting in this run-down spook concession—would you mind telling us exactly why you killed Daniel Manheim?"

"Oh, you've no doubt guessed that by now," said Willa. "I killed him because he had Nick Sanantonio killed."

"And you and Nick were sweethearts," said Groucho. "But I thought that was over."

"Nick and I were going to get back together," the actress told him. "All that bullshit about his going back to Dian didn't mean anything. Nick was like that, but it was me he really wanted again. Manheim ruined all that."

Groucho said, "So you killed him."

"Executed him, yes. The way you take care of a murderer."

I glanced over at Emily. "Why are you in on this?"

"Because I loved Nick, too."

Groucho asked, "And vice versa?"

"We'd better get on with this now," cut in Willa.

"Wait, wait, just a mo," said Groucho. "Satisfy my curiosity and tell us how you *knew* that Manheim was behind the gunning down of Nick Sanantonio."

The actress laughed. "What's your theory, Edgar Wallace?"

"Either somebody in Salermo's mob tipped you off, which is unlikely considering that you seem to have known before they did, or it was someone close to Manheim himself who—"

"C'mon," interrupted Emily, angry. "This is dragging on far too long, Willa."

"You're right, Em." From the pocket of her jacket she took an ordinary kitchen knife.

Holding up a cautionary hand, Groucho asked, "Could you two Valkyries hold on for a minute or two more?"

"What are you babbling about now?" asked Willa, gloved hand closing around the blade of the knife.

"It's only that I hear the World's Fair troopers sneaking up outside and getting ready to come charging in here," he explained. "I really would like to have them interrupt the festivities *before* rather than after you stab us."

"Shit." Emily sprinted out into the hallway. "He's probably bluffing, Willa."

Groucho gave Willa a sympathetic look. "You really didn't think that two such astute sleuths as Frank and myself would walk, all guileless, into such an obvious trap, did you, my dear?" he inquired. "I had a guide friend of mine alert the bobbies before we took a step out of the music pavilion."

Willa was about to reply when the rear door of the haunted house came slamming open.

Thirty-two

Hands on hips, Jane was surveying the suitcases lined up on the living room of our hotel suite. "I didn't buy that much stuff while we were here," she said forlornly. "And, you know, basically I don't like shopping."

"Relatively speaking," I said from the sofa.

"But here I am just about packed for the trip home and I've got enough left over to fill up another suitcase." She gestured at a pile of magazines, books, and Sunday comic sections, and a stack of folded blouses.

"Well, don't fret. Buy another suitcase if need be."

"That's sort of extravagant."

"We can afford to be extravagant, at least once."

She smiled, crossed over, sat beside me, and hugged me. "That's true, Frank," she said. "Everybody loves the *Hollywood Molly* radio show, mostly because of your terrific scripts, and it looks like we're guaranteed a whole season."

"What everybody loves, Jane, is your terrific characters," I said. "I merely fleshed them out a little."

After kissing me on the cheek, "Well, as a matter of fact, my comic strip characters are darn good," she admitted. "And I had as much to do with our radio success as you did."

"Since we've dropped the false modesty, I better confess that I think my scripts were sensational, too," I said. "The conclusion being that we're equally responsible for creating what looks to be a hit radio program and both deserve extra suitcases."

She hugged me once more before standing up. "And it's great that the advertising agency decided to produce the show out of their Los Angeles office," she said. "That way we can keep in closer touch with the production and you won't have to mail scripts here to Manhattan."

"Better radio actors in Hollywood, too."

"Maybe we can cast Dorgan as himself."

"And we could persuade him to give us a kickback on his salary."

Jane studied the collection of suitcases for a moment. "You won't take this the wrong way," she began, "but . . ."

"You want *two* more suitcases?"

"No. I was going to mention that I'm glad Groucho's not traveling home on the train to LA with us," she said. "He's a marvelous person, but . . . well, when you guys team up you inevitably seem to get bopped on the head somewhere along the way."

"That does appear to be a trend, yeah."

"This time you also nearly got murdered by Willa Jerome and her dippy secretary." She frowned, shaking her head. "They might have tossed you in a lagoon or a fountain, the way they did that drunken doctor."

"They didn't toss Dowling. He fell in after they stabbed him."

"Even so, when you're working on a case with him, I worry a heck of a lot that something terrible's going to happen to you."

"I appreciate that, Jane, but I can usually take care of myself."

"Then how come you get conked on the skull so often?" she asked. "By the way, was it Willa or Emily who sapped you this time?"

"They haven't made a full confession as yet."

"I'm not trying to curtail your detective career, mind you," my wife assured me. "Still and all, I hope it doesn't become any more frequent than it has been. And with Groucho staying on in Manhattan for a long run in *The Mikado* and us going back to Los Angeles, well, you can concentrate on your writing."

I cleared my throat. "Actually, my dear, Groucho won't be staying in New York."

"How can he play the Lord High Executioner on Broadway and not remain in town?"

"I haven't gotten around to telling you," I said, "but he telephoned while you were in the shower."

"And?"

"The backers of his version of *The Mikado* suffered some serious financial troubles and pulled out. The show won't be opening at all."

"That's awful for Groucho," she said. "Now he'll miss the chance to inflict Gilbert and Sullivan on a wider audience."

"He did sound somewhat downcast."

She eyed me, suspicion touching her face. "Wait now," she said, uneasy. "If he doesn't have to remain in New York . . . Frank, Groucho isn't coming back on the Super Chief with us, is he?"

I grinned. "Nope," I assured her. "He's staying in town a few more days and then flying home."

She exhaled, relieved. "Why's he hanging around in Manhattan?"

"For one thing, he promised Dian Bowers he'd attend the premiere of *Saint Joan*. She and Bill Washburn have gotten back together again and he also wants to wish them well, being in one of his avuncular moods apparently."

Jane sat in an armchair, tucking her legs under her. "Does that make for a happy ending—their getting together again?" she said. "From what you've told me, she was never particularly faithful to her husband, whatever name she was using."

"I don't know if you've noticed this, Jane, but not every woman in Hollywood is as trustworthy and faithful as you are. Oh, you might dance with a syndicate executive now and then, but basically—"

"Nuts to you," she mentioned.

Stretching up off the sofa, I wandered to the window to gaze down at Central Park across the way. "I think Groucho's also unhappy that there are some loose ends to the case."

"You caught the killers. What more does he want?"

"There's Hal Arneson, for one thing," I answered. "It's pretty obvious that he must've helped Manheim arrange for Nick Sanantonio's death. And Groucho has a hunch that Arneson may be the one who tipped Willa Jerome off to the fact that Manheim had her lover killed. But he probably won't ever be able to prove any of that."

"Frank, we're heading home tomorrow, no matter what. Aren't we?"

"We are, sure. I'm only telling you why Groucho is sticking around for a few more days."

She got up. "Let's go buy a suitcase," she said.

The premiere of *Saint Joan* was held at a movie palace nearly as large and opulent as Radio City Music Hall and less than two blocks to the west of it. The first person Groucho encountered when he went slouching backstage before the initial festivities was Conrad Nagel.

Noticing Groucho, the dapper actor hurried over to him. He adjusted the carnation in the lapel of his tuxedo, smiled uneasily, and said, "Well, Groucho, what brings you here?"

"An oxcart and, lord, what trouble we had getting it across the Brooklyn Bridge," he answered.

Nagel chuckled. "Always ready with the quip." He produced a crisp white handkerchief and wiped his brow.

"I'm also always ready with the Flit, so if you're having any problems with bugs or flying insects, give a holler, Connie."

"What I wanted to ask you, Groucho, was if—"

"Save your breath. I'm already promised to another."

"What I was concerned about was . . . are you planning to take part in tonight's premiere program? No one told me you were, yet here you are and if you're planning to interrupt my speech, I'd like to be alerted

208

in advance," said the actor. "I'll be reading a cablegram from George Bernard Shaw himself and—"

"Sent collect, no doubt," said Groucho.

"But are you intending any unexpected—"

"You can relax, old man. I merely popped back here to wish Dian and her husband well."

"You see, I still recall that time in Hollywood when you barged into my introduction at *The Pirate Prince* premiere and—"

"That was different, since I was in the midst of bringing a murderer to justice," explained Groucho.

"Yes, that's true. This time, from what I've been reading in the newspapers, you've already bagged your killers."

"Exactly, and to put your mind completely at ease, I promise to snooze during your entire introduction, Conrad my boy," said Groucho. "So unless I have a bout of sleepwalking, you're perfectly safe."

Looking, more or less, relieved, Nagel held out his hand. "A pleasure talking to you, Groucho," he said. "I hope your career takes a turn for the better soon."

"The same to you." He shook hands and moved on.

The door of Dian Bowers's temporary dressing room was partially open and as he approached, he overheard her talking to her husband. "Of course, it's permanent, Bill. We're together for good."

"I know, Nancy, but—"

"And no matter what you've heard, or read in the columns, dear, you know I was faithful to you the entire time we were separated."

Rolling his eyes slightly, Groucho walked on, deciding he'd look in on the happy couple a bit later in the evening. "What you have to keep in mind," he told himself, "is that actresses are good at acting."

"What the hell are you doing here?" Hal Arneson had come out of a backstage office and was glowering at Groucho.

"Spreading joy and good cheer," answered Groucho. "And you?"

"Okay, I know you caught Willa Jerome and Emily Collinson," said the publicity man. "That solved Dan Manheim's murder, but I still don't like you, buddy."

"Nor I you, now that we're letting our hair down," he said. "But, just as a favor, can you tell me what part you played in the killing of Nick Sanantonio?"

Arneson laughed, then glanced around. There was no one in the immediate vicinity. "Sure, since you can't prove a damn thing," he said, grinning. "Maybe I was aware of what Dan was up to and maybe I even knew some people who could do the job. Hell, it could be I even arranged jobs like that before for Manheim. Now try to do anything about it."

"No, I'm through with this case," Groucho told him. "It's only my curiosity I'm trying to satisfy now. So, one more thing, Arneson—did you tell Willa Jerome that Manheim was responsible for Sanantonio's death?"

Arneson looked away. "That would mean I gave her the reason to kill him," he said quietly. "If, say, I'd picked her up at a party just before we came back east and ended up spending the night with her, well, I might've talked too much, huh?" He shrugged. "As I advise a lot of my publicity clients to say, Groucho, 'No further comment.' "

"And as Charlie Chan often says, 'Thank you so much.' "

"Let's hope we don't run into each other again in the near future, Groucho." Arenson turned away.

"I'll see to that," promised Groucho.

Thirty-three

It rained the first two nights we were back home in Bayside and we didn't take Dorgan for his twilight walk until the evening of the third. The sky was overcast, the oncoming night sultry.

Our gift bloodhound, nose to the sand, gave the impression he was trailing somebody.

"Well, I suppose so," Jane was saying. It was her turn to manage the leash.

"Dogs aren't anywhere near as screwy as people," I reiterated. "Therefore, I repeat that I seriously doubt Dorgan was overly upset by our stay back in New York City."

"Our protracted stay," she said. "And I don't know, he seems extra mopey these past few days."

"He's a bloodhound. Bloodhounds are mopey-looking by nature," I said. "Has something to do with heredity and Mendelian laws."

"And right now he's snuffling along the beach, pretending to be a bloodhound and—"

"He *is* a bloodhound," I reminded.

"Sure, but we aren't a posse and we're not tracking an escaped murderer."

We were a few yards from the Bayside Diner when our dog gave out a gratified yowl and began tugging Jane in that direction.

"Hey, no dogs allowed in there, remember?" she said.

But Dorgan was determined to reach the place.

"Maybe Enery's on duty tonight and he'll fix him a burger to eat out here," I suggested, trotting in their wake.

When he reached the screen door of the diner, Dorgan went up on his hind legs, pressed his front paws against the jamb, and commenced howling.

"Hush," advised Jane.

The door was opened from within. "Goodness gracious me, a body can't hear himself think with all this unseemly noise out here." Groucho looked out at us. "Usually the sound I hear when I'm thinking is a melodious *plink plink,* although now and then it's more an *oompah oompah.* The point being, kiddies, that your odious hound is interrupting the process with his baleful caterwauling."

Jane said, "What the heck are you doing here?"

"I first dropped by your cottage and found you out," he replied. "I came here next, hoping against hope that you'd eventually turn up at your favorite haunt."

"We were taking Dorgan for a walk," I said.

"A likely story. You've probably been luring merchant ships to their doom on our rockbound coast and then looting them for rum."

"Well, that, too." Jane tied Dorgan to a low nearby post. "Stay here, boy, and we'll bring you a snack in a few minutes."

The dog produced a gurgling whimper.

"You don't want to get too close to Mr. Marx, do you, Dorgan? You know his scent makes you sneeze."

The bloodhound subsided, settling himself into a patient waiting position on the weedy sand.

Enery McBride was behind the counter, consulting a thick cookbook he had opened in front of him. "Welcome back," he said to Jane and me. Now that he was acting fairly regularly in the movies, he only worked occasional nights at our neighborhood diner. "And congratulations on landing the radio show."

"How'd you know about the *Hollywood Molly* deal?" I leaned an elbow on the counter.

"It was in *Variety* and on Johnny Whistler," he answered. "Oh, and I think Leo Haskell had an item in his column, although I'm not quite sure what he was trying to say." He tilted his head in Groucho's direction. "I think I can do it."

"What's he going to try to make for you?" Jane asked.

"Blintzes." Groucho returned to the booth where he'd been waiting for us.

"They're pretty much like crêpes," decided Enery, shutting the cookbook and returning it somewhere under the counter. "You guys want an order, too?"

Jane shook her head. "Just cocoa for us, Enery."

He looked at me. "She makes all your food decisions now?"

"Yep, and also picks out my pajamas."

Jane said, "And a hamburger for Dorgan."

"He prefers cheeseburgers," said our friend.

"Cheese then."

When we were seated across the booth from Groucho, I asked him, "Any special reason for your running us to ground?"

He said, "I got a long-distance telephone call from Lieutenant Lewin of the New York constabulary, my dears."

"And?"

"It seems Hal Arneson was found shot dead in his Manhattan hotel room at approximately noon today."

"Jesus," I said, sitting up. "Somebody from Salermo's mob must've caught up with him."

"That's Herb Lewin's theory," Groucho said. "Though he doubts he'll ever be able to prove it."

Jane shivered, hugging herself. "I know Arneson was probably as guilty as Manheim," she said quietly. "But I'm scared by this vigilante stuff."

"You can call it that, true," said Groucho. "You can probably also call it poetic justice. Even though it doesn't rhyme."